By the same author

Frames of Mind

Heights of Folly

by

Philippa Bunting

The Pine Marten Press

First published in 2010

ISBN 978-0-9552199-2-4

Typeset and cover design by GSB (Edinburgh)

Printed and bound in Great Britain by
Lightning Source

For David

and in memory of Penkill Castle, which we tried so hard to save for the Nation. Penkill still stands. Its immensely important historic contents were dispersed in the 1990s.

In memory, too, of the rugged individualists who have kept, and still keep, the ideal of child-centred education alive.

Cave canem

Chapter 1

"Be modern, Mother." Tiffany delayed in front of the mirror, moving her head from side to side, intent on her image. The face looking back was alert, irregular, a little ungoverned. "Aunt Sylvia should have married. Someone tough but romantic, who could have given her children."

Beneath the bobbed hair Iona's expression hardened. "I am what you call modern. It seems you are rather old-fashioned, with your ideas of wedlock and romantic love. Do get off if you're going. I will expect you all back here by half past six." Turning to Tiffany's friend, a strikingly lovely girl, she asked her if she thought Tiffany had some odd ideas. The girl's name was Pippa Cursiter. Iona found her watchfulness rather disconcerting.

Tiffany, still at the mirror, drew back her hair, then loosened it again. "Make sure I'm properly awake in the morning, please. I'll go to the early service with you." Her eyes grew reflective. It was a faintly comical nose. Rather a narrow face. She was taller than her mother. "I'm too tall," she said, sounding more resigned than she felt. She was dissatisfied with her body. It always seemed to be her hands that dropped things, her feet that tripped.

The two young women sauntered up the drive. Azaleas, their leaves turning to deep, autumnal reds; mature trees; a half bend; a reverse bend: and there it was, the dramatic silhouette of Penwhapple Castle. "The bell up there is famous," said Tiffany, as they waited outside the nail-studded front door. "It tolled of its own accord when Rossetti tried to drown himself." She paused and added, "In 1869."

"So this is Penwhapple," was Pippa's dreamy reply. She rested a hand on her hip, exuding hazy charm. Her hair was fair, with richer depths. She wore it thick to her shoulders, held back with a velvet band.

"But I always leave it unlocked!" Sylvia cried, opening the door and clasping her niece in one grand gesture, appraising Pippa at the same time. They shoved the door to and, passing through a glazed inner door, mounted the broad turnpike, three abreast.

"Dear old mural," Tiffany exclaimed, referring to the scenes of mediaeval chivalry with which the stairwell was decorated. Her pleasure was sharpened by the presence of her impassive friend.

"Vulnerable old mural," Sylvia rejoined. "You see how the lettering has deteriorated? I knew we shouldn't have had central heating put in."

They went into the kitchen, with its old cooker. There was more of what Sylvia called "lettering" on the cupboards. She stumped about making tea and finding cake. She and Iona were both tall, with the same open, handsome faces. Guileless eyes. Heavy limbs. "Wait a minute, what's the time?" Her gaze turned to the clock. "You've probably had tea already? I'd no idea it was so late." Her straight, grey hair swung with her movements. It was cut in a bob, like her sister's.

"We'd love some tea. No cake, perhaps. You've not forgotten about dinner?"

"Half past six. Plenty of time for some cake." Sylvia thought it a shame her sister had had to share Tiffany's first afternoon at home with Pippa. She had taken a dislike for her visitor, she realised.

Tiffany carried the tea tray up to the library. This left Sylvia free to comment on the scenes from the King's Quair, as the mural was called. Because she felt her thoughts about Pippa had been rather negative - a serious lapse - Sylvia explained the identities of the individuals portrayed there in more than her usual detail.

"Who is that?" asked Pippa, pointing to a figure whose long hair and diaphanous garments undulated round her like the baluster of a glass chalice.

"Now, that is almost certainly Bryony herself, Sholto's sister. Important to you, of course, as the founder of Somersby School." Sylvia paused, as if wanting to be absolutely fair. "Or it could just be Christina Rossetti. She was a regular visitor, and Sholto was fond of her. She gave him that sundial you may have noticed outside."

They talked their way to the library. "How's the gardening going?" Tiffany asked. "Not too stiff to tackle the ravine?"

"Very stiff. There are various accidents waiting in that area."

"Couldn't a party from the school have a go at it?"

"Possibly. They'll have to be supervised. I rather enjoy directing operations, as a matter of fact. Bit like you in that respect."

Pippa was examining the vaulted ceiling. Close beneath the cornice ran a gothic script. Wild. Illusions. Fly. Something. Fancy. Had. Something. Conceived.

There was a good deal of decorative carving. On the huge stone fireplace. Around the windows. On the panels of the cupboard, which Sylvia said was the original front door. The plaster had an inconclusive, papery look, as if all that baronial self-confidence was a sham.

"Have you had any more lapses?" Tiffany inquired, with the directness of youth but in tones suggesting great fondness for her aunt.

"Oh yes. I depend on my lapses."

"According to Uncle Lionel yours is the last flowering of the Moffat clairvoyance." Tiffany kept a straight face, glancing at Pippa.

Sylvia was unruffled. She placed her expensive old shoes close together, tugging the corduroy skirt tight across her knees. "Take some cake, both of you. Lionel is the last person to understand such matters."

Her guests did as they were told. Worn leather, antiquarian gleanings of carved oak, paintings by Sholto, Bryony and their Pre-Raphaelite friends. The gunloops where jackdaws had made nests, year after year. The fire irons which were said to have been a gift from Holman Hunt. Tiffany tried sinking lower in her chair, becoming more uncomfortable. She would have been better off sitting at the library table, another of Sholto's antiquarian finds.

Pippa reached for some cake. She ate it slowly, as though preoccupied with her surroundings without being much moved by them.

Tiffany said, "You're looking well, Aunt Sylvia. But the arthritis still bothers you?"

"It always will. There's no cure, although rosemary compresses help a little. They'll never persuade me to leave the castle. I tell you that now, in case your mother drops any of her famous hints this evening. They'll have to carry me out feet first. That's what I tell your Uncle Drummond."

"How reassuring for him."

"Well, your mother wouldn't tell you so herself, but she's almost completely deaf in her left ear. And you know that Drummond has been through another bad patch? Your Mother may not mention that either." Tiffany chewed her fingertip, fearing to hear more, while Pippa's expression became dreamier than ever. She had long since decided she would never work out which of the Moffats was which. "I tell you this," Sylvia concluded, "because I know no-one else will. The other lung is shadowy too."

Before Tiffany could respond, Pippa intervened, remarking that nettles were good for arthritis. Tiffany made herself laugh. "Do try them, dear aunt." She turned to her friend. "So, what do you think of Penwhapple? Can you imagine it revamped by wealthy yuppies?"

Pippa considered. "Yes, I can. It could be stunning."

Tiffany caught the look on her aunt's face. Forcing herself to sit up, she toyed with the teapot. "So Uncle Drummond still enjoys life?"

"He doesn't know what it is to give in. Still active in the firm, and a splendid Chairman of the Trustees of Somersby."

Tiffany turned back to Pippa. "Drummond's the elder of my two uncles. Lionel's the younger one, Ricky's father. Rather sarcastic, embittered by divorce." Glancing slyly at her aunt she went on, still addressing her friend, "Rather sinister, actually."

"Really, Tiffany, that's a bit steep," Sylvia objected.

Tiffany stretched her long legs and got to her feet, asking if she could use the phone.

"You look like a giant spider in those black velvet trews," Pippa told her.

Pulling a face, Tiffany said, "Ricky might just not have headed for the pub yet."

"Do use the phone by all means. Take your time. Pippa can be telling me how she's settling in at Somersby."

Pippa brightened up, and began expounding her views on education.

When Tiffany came back into the room it was Sylvia who was speaking. "'Teach integrity to the children entrusted to your care, from the earliest age. They must all find their own truth." She spoke with sing-song emphasis. "I can hear Bryony saying that, all those years ago."

"I dread even mentioning the subject," Tiffany remarked, "but of all the paintings in the castle, the one I'd treasure most would be the double portrait. Bryony and Sholto. Of course, everyone will be squabbling for it."

"Everyone will not," Sylvia affirmed. "Moving that picture would be the height of folly. I do not mince my words."

"You'll be thinking all this is somewhat recondite." Tiffany laughed, compelling Pippa to meet her eye. "I'm just nipping down to the hall." she went on. "Come on, I'll show you. I like seeing everything. It's funny how you can know a place so well, yet forget."

"Just a look then," was Pippa's reply.

They descended to the banqueting hall. The bell which Tiffany had pointed out stood on a buttress to this crow-stepped, Victorian addition, under its own assertive little bell house. Pippa saw a light, high raftered hall, a cross between a chapel and a gymnasium, she thought. It was panelled with narrow planks above a frieze of wallpaper. The walls were covered with pictures, large ones up high, smaller ones against the frieze. The passage linking the hall to the tower was decorated with coarsely embroidered tapestry. There was more gothic lettering for her to decipher: 'Some. Moral. Truth. In. Fiction's. Veil.' The light from the large windows made it easier to read this inscription than the one upstairs.

Tiffany embarked on a rapid commentary to which Pippa only half listened. "That's the Penwhapple burn. Sholto painted it every summer. It was a special place, where he and Bryony renewed their love for each other."

"But I thought they were brother and sister!"

"I don't mean sex. They don't 'do' sex at Somersby, as you'll find out for yourself – I don't think!"

Pippa glanced at the small painting of someone walking in a garden, with a dog. 'Fogo,' was it? The family name for all their dogs. "Did you catch your cousin?" she asked, swinging round.

"No, I'll have to try again from Mum's. Looks as if we may not get him this weekend."

Upstairs, the telephone rang. They could hear Sylvia moving across to answer, then her voice calling from the stairs. It was Iona. "She wonders if we'll be down soon. Supper at half past six."

"Really, Mother is an organising person," Tiffany said. "I'll nip on ahead if you don't mind. She may like some help at this point. Blast! You haven't seen the Rossetti, Pippa. Our most famous picture."

Pippa was much more disappointed not to be seeing the famous Ricky.

By the time they sat down to one of Iona's candlelit, vegetarian meals it was well after seven. The main course was salmon, which counted as a vegetable in Iona's system. Before Sylvia walked back to the castle the sisters had their usual confabulation over commissions executed and trifling sums of money spent.

"You certainly do not owe me two pounds thirty," Iona declared. She sounded almost scornful. "I asked you to buy all that fruit and I'm sure I never gave you enough. I probably owe you at least three pounds. Now, what about the smoked salmon we shared?"

"Well, leave it now. We'll square up another time." Sylvia shouldered into her jacket.

"Do take this. I'd rather settle it now." Iona thrust a five pound note into her sister's hand. It was Sylvia's turn to look put out.

She let it pass. "I'll tell you what I owe you tomorrow."

It was late by the time Tiffany accompanied Pippa the short distance to her quarters at Somersby School. Iona heard them laughing as they let themselves out, and Tiffany saying, "I do not mince my words! It would be the height of folly!"

When morning came, Tiffany could not be roused. Iona went to the early service alone.

Chapter 2

Soon after two o'clock the visitors who had been wandering over the grounds at Somersby began to converge on the main hall. It was a fine October day, warm enough for the doors to be left standing open.

Somersby took its name from a Georgian farmhouse. Most of the classrooms were in what had been agricultural buildings, known as the bullock sheds. Behind them, on a slight rise, was the art room and, behind that, Camelot, an oddly shaped, wooden construction, where visitors were now congregating. Further away, screened by trees and nearer the road, was a neat row of Victorian cottages, now converted into a girls' dormitory. It was here that Pippa had her quarters.

Gwen Moffat drove into the car park, switched off the engine and glanced at Drummond. "Well, that was a lovely drive."

Drummond stirred himself and clambered slowly out. Fogo leaped after him. Drummond produced an expanding leash from his pocket and, attaching it to Fogo's collar, found it instantly whirled to a distance of several yards. Fogo whipped behind a tree. Drummond, retrieving him and retracting rapidly, became entangled with the lead around his legs.

Gwen hastened to the rescue. "Not such a wonderful invention, really." She had never thought it was, but Drummond saw it as a great asset.

"Don't fuss, Gwen." Briskly Drummond returned Fogo to the car and the lead to a jacket pocket. Gwen adjusted the windows and locked up. Drummond squared his shoulders, consciously assuming the part of Chairman of the Trustees. His jacket was of apple green tweed, overchecked in darker green and an almost purple brown. A proper man's cloth, weighing a good twenty-four ounces.

"We're not going to do a lot of standing this afternoon," Gwen told him. "It's not worth it."

"I'll be all right," Drummond asserted, following her towards the house. No-one spoke quite like Gwen, soft, light, seemingly indulgent. A cultivated voice, defining her as the product of an exclusive Edinburgh girls'school.

"Now, when you see Tiffany, don't go overboard with delight," Gwen murmured, as they skirted a lively group of families. He always made too much of his niece, was too attentive, ready to interrupt whatever he was doing and leap to his feet.

"Not overboard. Just pleased."

"And you won't mention money. The subject of Wills is becoming a morbid preoccupation."

"Right." Drummond allowed himself a hint of satire.

"You favouritise her over Ricky. It could be quite hurtful, perhaps not to Ricky but, in a different way, to Lionel."

"Right!" Drummond made it a more straightforward assertion this time, conscious that Gwen was talking nonsense. It was Ricky whom he favouritised. Despite the problems the boy had had with his professional qualifications, he and Lionel had always expected Ricky to take over the family business. It had only recently dawned on Drummond that, of the two cousins, Tiffany was the more able.

They stopped on the gravel forecourt, where they had arranged to meet the Headmaster, Ogier Boyd. As usual, Gwen had made them a shade early. Boys on bikes were doing handbrake skids, sending pebbles spurting. Drummond raised his stick in jovial greeting.

Gwen took his elbow as they approached the steps. She complemented him in her emerald costume, the hem a shade high over her neat knees. With her light brown hair tucked into a French pleat she was, in her mid-forties, still a girl in Drummond's eyes, both rounded and slim.

From the inner hall Ogier himself materialised, wearing his best kilt. "Marvellous! You're here. Sylvia is the only other Trustee who has made it. I'll take you straight to Camelot. I shall be sounding off in approximately. . . . ten and a half minutes?" He ran his hand through rumpled, sandy hair. "Do take the seats we've reserved for you in the front row. They're upholstered!"

As Drummond eased himself into his chair and Gwen arranged her tight-skirted person on another, Tiffany hailed them. "Tiffany, my dear!" Drummond lost no time in hauling himself up. "How are you? Looking ever more.... " Mindful of Gwen's presence, he substituted 'healthy' for 'glamorous.' "Come and sit with us. Is Iona with you?"

"Yes, and Sylvia. We're sitting several rows back."

Drummond turned and waved. With Sylvia and Iona was Miss Spencer, "Ogier's right hand man" according to Lionel. Formidable authority emanated from Samantha Spencer. Equally palpable was the aura around Drummond's elder sister, still widely regarded as the embodiment of the school's ideals. Drummond felt a pang of regret for something lurking beyond the edge of his satisfaction. "Do sit down, Tiffany," he insisted. "You make me uneasy, standing over us like that. Tell us who that new teacher is. She looks set to grace the occasion."

It was thus that Tiffany found herself sitting with Drummond in the middle of the front row. While Tiffany provided an enthusiastic thumbnail sketch of her friend Pippa Cursiter, Gwen studied the pictures on the walls. Representations of the Parsifal legend, they were executed in veils of watercolour, and were in crudely carved frames. Had the pictures been more orthodox, Gwen's approach to yet another Somersby festival might have been friendlier.

Camelot itself was understated, a place of spatial harmony, its dome painted a translucent blue. Ogier appeared, his hair smoother. He began with the familiar formula: "Dear Children, dear Parents, dear Teachers." Then he delivered one of the cryptic addresses in which he specialized, reassuringly familiar to those who knew Somersby, puzzling to those who did not. Michaelmas, said Ogier, was like childhood, a season of balance. Balance between hot and cold, wet and dry, calm and storm. A season of meteors, of the Heavenly Iron. A season of joyful anticipation, when a great Archangel beckoned. A modern education needed to strengthen wills, to create confidence, to understand knowledge as unity. For this year's Festival the children would show the part played by rhythmic activity in the classroom.

For Tiffany, an old girl of the school, Ogier's talk was engagingly commonplace. For Drummond, it was bold. Outwardly conventional himself, Drummond liked the way Somersby challenged received wisdom. Pippa, sitting near Ogier on the stage, looked as if butter wouldn't melt in her mouth.

Ogier brought his address to a close, then raised a hand.

"Before I invite Class Four to come forward, may I just welcome our new English teacher? She is Pippa Cursiter, and we feel sure her contribution will be a happy one for her and the children she will work with."

To Tiffany's surprise, and as clapping broke out, Pippa rose to her feet. It was clear she intended to speak. Tiffany held her breath.

"Thank you very much, Mr Boyd . . . all of you here . . . " Pippa glanced from Ogier to the nearer faces with studied calm. "I look forward to working with you and sharing my enthusiasms. Perhaps I shall be able to take part in the School Festival myself next year, with some of my pupils. I do hope so."

Smiling only at this point, and with modesty, Pippa sat down again. Ogier nodded in her direction and lost no time in urging a group of eleven-year-olds to recite 'Young Lochinvar.' They belted it out with virile self-assurance.

Successive groups of children now demonstrated their skills in corporate rhythm. They chanted ballads. They loudly shouted the arithmetic tables, stamping them in geometric forms. They sang songs in three languages. A select group of older pupils performed eurythmy. The festival concluded with an anthem written by Bryony Moffat. It had a mediaeval conceit and a rousing chorus: 'Live pure. Speak true. Right wrong. Follow the King.' Lionel couldn't bear it.

"I"m a bit concerned about your Aunt Sylvia," Drummond told Tiffany, taking her arm. "I expect your Mother will have spoken to you by now about our ideas for the castle. Penwhapple is full of things associated with members of the Pre-Raphaelite circle. There are one or two items of considerable value. And then there is the archive. Lionel and I are agreed we need help. Your aunt is unreceptive. Why? What does she want with all that responsibility, and the stairs, and the cold?"

Tiffany did not like to admit that Iona had told her nothing. "Well, Penwhapple's not cold, at least not as Sylvia sees it. She actually dislikes the central heating. It isn't any old castle, you know. It's fairly modernised and snug and small."

"She's not a wonderful sixty-year-old any more," said Drummond. "Although we all treat her as if she is. Try and enthuse her with a labour-saving flat."

Gwen noticed that he was looking about him with what she

recognised as the Moffat 'private agenda' expression on his face. "What's the matter? What's happening now?" she inquired.

Drummond half turned away. "I just want to get hold of . . ."

"You want what? I thought we were all invited to take tea now."

It was her obstructionist tone. Drummond turned to Tiffany. "Could you kindly find young Miss Cursiter? I like to make myself known to any new members of staff as soon as possible."

"Are you not ready to sit down?" objected Gwen briskly.

But Drummond was already extending an arm. "Miss Cursiter? As a very old friend of Somersby School I am delighted to make your acquaintance. Drummond Moffat."

Pippa, led forward by Tiffany, was clasping Drummond's hand when Ogier joined them. She stepped back abruptly, giving her full attention to the Headmaster. It was Drummond who took up the slack. "Not one of our strengths in the past," he remarked to Ogier, "Somersby French. But those young people did wonders with Le Petit Prince."

Before Ogier could reply, Pippa addressed him. "Thank you for introducing me this afternoon. I'd like to second what Mr Moffat has said about Le Petit Prince. There's one point I feel I ought to mention . . . ?" She tilted her head to one side, suggestive both of judgment and diffidence.

Good heavens, what now? Tiffany wondered. Her Aunt Gwen seemed spell-bound by the young woman.

"Yes?" said Ogier. "Go ahead."

Pippa spoke in a fluent, matter-of-fact voice. "What I was thinking is this. Do you not believe children achieve more when the sexes are segregated? I realise that this must seem a heretical view. But there is a good deal of evidence that the sexes function better separately, even at very early ages, when they are free from what I see as psychological distractions."

Gwen thought, yes, I do agree.

Ogier was nodding slowly. "Somersby did of course start as a girls' school. Then, in Sylvia Moffat's time, an impulse for renewal found expression in what was seen as a more holistic approach. This was a courageous decision and one that has been widely imitated. I can't see us ever segregating again." He met Pippa's gaze for a moment, with an encouraging smile. Pippa did not return it. Tiffany felt uncomfortably that Ogier's lightness of touch, conveyed with exactly the right element of respect, was being repulsed. Having ignored her uncle, it seemed Pippa was determined to patronise Ogier as well.

Gwen took possession of Drummond's arm. "I attended an all-girls school and I am thankful I did. One has only to read accounts of bullying in the papers, quite apart from the league tables. I'm a feminist in this respect I'm afraid." She was successful in drawing a demure smile from Pippa. "But why don't we all go through for some tea together? You deserve it, Ogier." Resolutely she led them towards the Mansion, as the old farm house was called. Pippa did not go with them but made her way to the art room, where she was on duty. Tiffany was to join her there in due course.

It was getting late by the time Tiffany pushed through the art room door into warmth and diffused light. The place was tidier than usual, with a selection of handiwork on the big trestle table. The walls were covered with watercolours, a Somersby trademark. For the festival a selection had been made, demonstrating the progression from simple, two-colour exercises, as taught to the juniors, to the complex work of the upper school.

For a moment Tiffany felt a pang of disappointment at how uniform the work appeared. The previous year's fifth-formers had been given Rossetti's The Mystic Marriage of Saint George as their project. In Tiffany's fifth year it had been Sir Galahad at the Ruined Chapel. She had earned high praise for capturing the way light fell on Sir Galahad's face. Mrs Hogarth had said that the picture conveyed an "inner experience" of light.

"The Scholar Returns." It was not Pippa, or Mrs Hogarth, who welcomed her with this gnomic utterance, but Samantha Spencer. "I've asked your friend Miss Cursiter to look for a missing child. How did you enjoy the festival? Your friend conducted herself with distinction, I thought."

"She did, rather."

"Glad to hear you've been conducting yourself with distinction too. One success after another. We're getting quite proud."

"This is good," said Tiffany, picking up an exercise in mirror drawing. A knot from the Book of Kells had been loosely reproduced and reinterpreted.

"Yes, that's Phoebe Donaldson's work. She's talented. We're

thinking of giving Phoebe's class Into Battle for their fifth year project."

The door squeaked and a small crowd entered, Pippa, Sylvia, Iona and a group of unconnected visitors. Pippa was in charge of a small, unruly boy. This was Antony Hogarth, an adorable five-year-old with hair so fair and angelic he seemed unreal. His mother was the art teacher who had praised Tiffany's work, his father the school handyman. The latter had given up his job that autumn and gone off without notice, causing considerable disruption.

"Apparently he's expecting to spend tonight at Penwhapple with Miss Moffat," Pippa informed Samantha.

The small boy appealed to Sylvia. "Can we go?"

"Of course. Get your pyjamas and we'll be off."

"You have to think of the work it would give Miss Moffat," Iona told him, "not just of yourself."

"Fiddlesticks. He's no work at all," Sylvia asserted. "We're old friends. We'll be good for each other."

"Perhaps Tiffany should stay with you until he's in bed."

"On her last night home?" Sylvia swept the idea aside. "You'll only be two minutes away if anything crops up." She looked at Iona and laughed robustly. "I can't think why you want to change an arrangement that was made days ago."

"Come on, Mum," said Tiffany. "Of course I'll help out if needed. Pippa and I will fetch his night things." Smiling down at Antony, she missed her mother's look of annoyance.

Tiffany, Pippa and Antony went off, Antony incandescent with excitement. The others waited for the pyjamas to arrive.

Chapter 3

Drummond watched Gwen talking to his sisters, 'the young plants of grace,' as he fondly imagined them. He felt pleased with the way he had negotiated the stairs. The meeting had gone well. Trust Lionel to dub the idea of getting help from the Royal Museum as 'The National Solution.' Still, Sylvia had agreed. He supposed that was progress. He let the womenfolk get on with serving tea in their own way.

Returning to her seat, Iona stumbled. She went down heavily on one side between the sofa and an oak chair, narrowly missing a brass kettle and stand. Gwen saw the danger from a selfish point of view, glad that Iona had not been holding the tea tray.

Lionel, slight and agile, was the first to the spot. Iona was already struggling to her feet. Sylvia, with visions of a broken hip, bent over her sister, anxious to help. She and Lionel steadied her as she regained both balance and composure, attempting to laugh off the incident.

"No, I'm all right, really I am. So stupid of me to trip over, I can't think how it happened."

"All too easily," was Lionel's sardonic rejoinder.

Iona's flush deepened. "I suppose it was that little stool. Small things like that can be quite dangerous."

"I'll put it away." Sylvia was mortified. "There's no need for a stool there. Are you sure you're safe to walk? No damage done?"

"Perfectly certain." Iona could not bear to admit to any sort of threat to her independence. She particularly disliked a loss of dignity. Hence the tartness of her voice.

"It would be sacrilege to banish the stool," said Lionel. "It was probably a present from Dante Gabriel Rossetti himself. Sholto's ghost might ring the great bell, or barking sound forth from the watchtower."

"Of course it can be moved if it's liable to cause an accident."

Sylvia got up. "I'm going to fetch the arnica."

"I really am all right. Just a slight bump on this thigh. I think I went down rather gracefully." Iona subsided on the sofa. Sylvia found the arnica and watched Iona squeeze several drops into her mouth.

"Do I gather you've had the little boy up for the night again? Ant?" Gwen put the name in inverted commas, glancing at Lionel. He raised his eyebrows at her, very slightly.

"He comes quite often now. It's difficult for his mother to have him at Somersby all the time, with her teaching and the father not there. He's spending tonight as well."

"Don't tell me he's here now?"

"Yes, as a matter of fact. He's having a story in the kitchen with Annie. All that rushing around stopped long ago."

"You get tired I expect," Lionel observed. His fair hair was slicked close to his head, making him appear sharp and inquisitive. "You were tempted by a cherub and found you had a little demon."

"What nonsense! He's a nice child. It helps everyone if I can have him and he's so happy here."

"You'll be worn out, going up and down those stairs," Iona said, sealing her recovery by going on the attack. "Let him come to me tonight. He can go back to Somersby tomorrow. That will have been long enough."

"You're certainly not to think of having him. That would be ridiculous, when you've had a fall. You'd be better coming here for a night yourself and giving your leg a rest."

"But there's nothing whatever the matter with it! I've told you, I'm perfectly all right, thank you." Emotionally more explicit than her sister, Iona flushed again, less with gratitude than exasperation.

"I'll drop him off on my way home," said Lionel. "Let's have no unnecessary drama over the boy."

"Well, that would be a silly thing to do, when I've specially arranged with his mother to have him for a second night."

"Gwen and I could take him," put in Drummond. "I'd like a word with Ogier about school business. We could suggest that that new teacher, Tiffany's friend, could make herself useful."

"Oh for goodness sake, don't you dare suggest any such thing!" Iona expostulated, going even pinker. "As if Pippa Cursiter hasn't enough to do, learning the ropes at her new job." Her brothers and sister seemed determined to touch every tender spot in her self-esteem.

"Don't be put-upon." Lionel gave both his sisters a vinegary smile. "Miss Cursiter isn't too busy to go out pubbing with Ricky and Tiffany every weekend."

Iona eased her stiff thigh surreptitiously. "Yes, and you've had us all up for a meal twice now, Sylvia. Lionel's right. We take Penwhapple for granted. We've loved coming here. But the work has fallen on you. I'm so glad we were able to start thinking about the future this afternoon." As a risk worth taking, she concluded, "You only need to trip on those awful stone stairs and imagine the consequences! You saw how easily it happened to me."

Drummond nodded towards Lionel, securing his attention on their elder sister. "Do, first of all, try to be helpful to the experts from the Royal Museum. We must get the contents properly evaluated. There's nothing threatening in that."

The door creaked. A small boy with a shock of fair hair was regarding them with a winsome expression. "I am staying here." He seemed unsure if he was enunciating a fact or suppressing a query.

Iona and Sylvia exchanged rapid glances. "You're staying here for a second night," said Sylvia. "Then back to Mummy and your friends at school."

"Are you sure you won't let me take him tonight? It's ridiculous for you to wear yourself out." In her mind Iona had already established Antony's sleeping quarters at her own little house. Tiffany would find him there when she arrived back from Edinburgh. He was a nice enough child.

"He's no trouble," Sylvia replied stoutly. "If Tiffany gets back in time perhaps she could help put him to bed."

"We wanted to be home in good time, remember." Gwen tilted her head at Drummond, giving her remark an ulterior depth. Her husband looked baffled but did not contradict.

Lionel stood up. "I must look in on the office before we close. Tidy up the chaos created by the Meteor of the North."

Gwen gave him a smile. "Really and truly, Lionel, you are always so sarcastic about Ricky."

Lionel's shoulders twitched in irritable deprecation. "Oh, as to that, I speak as the Proud Father."

"I always knew Ricky would do well in the office. He's good

with people," Iona said. She pulled herself upright, hoping her smile would mask the ache down her side. Sylvia followed them to the door. The sisters sensed that they had been the elected butts of the occasion.

"Thank you for a splendid tea. And thank you for being sensible, dear Sylvia. We must think of the time when you can no longer manage here, as Iona says. We owe it to the young people." Drummond refused to let Gwen take his arm. If he felt dizzy he would pretend to examine the King's Quair again. Family councils in the banqueting hall would be followed by tea in the library for years yet.

"Next time perhaps we'll have tea in the banqueting hall," said Sylvia, as Antony seized her hand. "Save ourselves the stairs."

"If you'd like to come to my little house, it's the one just down the drive," Iona told Antony. "I've got some stuffed animals you could play with." The little boy wrinkled his nose and shrank behind Sylvia. "Careful!" Iona exclaimed, rather more brusquely than she had intended. "Don't pull Miss Moffat over."

Tiffany arrived from Edinburgh earlier than usual. Iona sent her straight up to the castle, where she provoked a high degree of excitement in Antony by starting a game of catch. Sylvia reluctantly stopped them, enjoying the sound of laughter but fearing another fall. "Did you get a chance to speak to your Mother before coming up?" she asked.

Tiffany tickled Antony a last time and stood panting. "Not really. She said I was to come up straight away."

"I ask, because she slipped over this afternoon. Fell heavily on one side. I suspect she's quite badly bruised, but she'll never admit more than she need."

"Oh dear, and I've said I'll go out this evening with Pippa." Tiffany's consternation was genuine enough and lasted until she got home.

"Mum, I hear you went crashing down at tea this afternoon. Sylvia sounded quite worried. Are you OK?"

"As you can see, I'm as mobile as ever. Nothing whatever the matter. Does it suit you if we eat in a bit less than half an hour? Or would that be altogether too countrified?" She was gratified when Tiffany complained she was famished and wanted to eat at once.

Over dinner Iona attempted to explain the National Solution to her daughter. Drummond's idea was that Penwhapple's historic contents would be acquired by the Royal Museum and lent back for permanent display. The money raised would be used on the upkeep of the fabric.

"Another way would be for me and Ricky to get married," said Tiffany. "Can you see me married to Ricky? We could take the cares of running Penwhapple off you all."

"Hardly reason to marry Ricky." The feelings Tiffany had for Ricky were indeed rather desperate, Iona reflected, since it was plain he did not reciprocate her interest. Tiffany would no doubt grow out of the attachment. She had always been a slow developer. That was the trouble with Somersby. The school deliberately held its pupils back. The theory was that they would mature all the more strongly later. "I can't see you and Ricky making a life together anywhere, let alone up there." Iona gestured in the direction of the castle. "Besides, what about your famous career?"

"Seriously, d'you think we aren't suited?"

"Do you think you are?"

Tiffany wrinkled her nose, stretched her arms above her head and uttered a loud guffaw. She did not reply. Iona got up and scraped the remnants of food off her daughter's plate.

Sitting on the edge of the bed, Sylvia was showing Antony one of Sholto Moffat's brown-wash drawings. It depicted the Wise and Foolish Virgins at the Bridegroom's Door. Like everything else at Penwhapple it had extensive historical and aesthetic associations. In this case the most important was Saint Sebald's church in Nuremberg. Sholto and Bryony had gone there to pursue their studies into Christian mysticism, an interest which had led in due course to the foundation of Somersby. The little picture had been drawn from the balcony of Dürer's house.

"I feel sorry for those ones," said Antony, pointing to the luckless girls shut out from the bridal chamber.

Sylvia's heart gladdened. "That's just how I always felt. Perhaps they found their way to an open door in the end."

"I don't think they did," the boy said sadly.

Sylvia persuaded him it was time to go to sleep. She told him the story of Parsifal, the Holy Fool, much her favourite of the Knights of the Round Table. He had persevered, completed his quest and "found the open door."

Long before she could finish, Antony's eyes had closed.

Chapter 4

The weather had been agreeably mild for much of the Spring Term. As Ogier got ready for his afternoon tour of inspection, he decided that Samantha was right. There was a need for a new pioneering phase. Smiling to himself, he found he was looking forward to checking the bicycle workshop. Someone had been putting tools back wrong. He intended to get a grip on the situation.

The moment he stepped from the front door he heard ominous yells from the play area behind the Mansion. A treehouse overlooked the old farm pond. From it a steel hawser ran to the sycamore on the far bank, carrying a trapeze. As he rounded the corner Ogier saw Robert, one of the older boys, encouraging a group of youngsters to drop into the pond. Before he could move, Ogier realised that intervention would not be necessary. Someone else was on the scene. A shout of "immediately" rang across the play area. Specific orders followed, in which the words "drying room" featured. Robert was held back for more detailed remonstrance. Ogier quietly withdrew.

He was checking the cycle repair shelves, with their neatly labelled boxes, when a shaft of light warned him that someone had come through the door behind him. He turned sharply. It was Pippa, in an aureole of spring sunshine.

"Four of the junior boys and one senior have been swinging over the pond. According to their story one of them accidentally fell in. By the time I heard the shouts, Robert was on the scene and every last one of them was soaking. Except Robert, of course."

"Do you want me to speak to them?"

"Everything's under control, thank you. You know what I think about Robert's influence."

"I'm sure you handled it all. You've sorted out clean clothes, and the - drying room?"

"Everything."

"Well done. But do let me speak to Robert. It must not appear that you have a down on him."

"He is simply rather unfortunate. I would like you to speak to him, but not about this. I wish you would tell him to get rid of those ferrets."

"Has there been trouble with the ferrets, then?"

"No actual trouble. But he's still rather threatening with them."

"If there's been a problem I'll take it up. But, you know, on the general issue, Robert has looked after his ferrets well. In fact, having them has been a positive experience. By all means raise the question of pets at the next College meeting. I've felt for some time that we should be reviewing the rather ad hoc practice that has been allowed to build up."

"The ferrets have such ugly habits. Robert feeds them dead rabbits, with the skins still on."

"Surely they're rather clean little animals."

"He does such revolting things with them."

"What things?"

"Putting them down the loos!"

The mouth which formulated this accusation was so charming that Ogier's reaction could have seemed satirical. "You'll be laughed out of court if you try that old chestnut on the College," he told her.

She responded with a level gaze. Pets, Ogier reflected, were a dangerous topic.

As Ogier entered the art room he thought for a moment that Pippa had preceded him. Phoebe Donaldson, the latest in a succession of gifted pupils, sat beside Alison Hogarth at the trestle table, deeply absorbed in her work.

"Look at what she's been doing. Do show your fifth year project to Mr Boyd, Phoebe."

Phoebe turned towards him and smiled. She kept her eyes averted, as if she was afraid she might giggle. The watercolour on which she was working was of a knight kneeling before a young woman.

Ogier examined it for some moments, surprised by the feelings it evoked. "You've copied this from Before the Battle, I take it?"

"Yes," said Alison, coming to the rescue of the tongue-tied Phoebe. She was dumpy, with straight, dark hair, unlike Antony, who resembled his father. "Compare it with the original. Phoebe has caught something quite special." She pushed across the reproduction from which Phoebe had been working.

Ogier said, "It's a beautiful image." Smiling again at Phoebe, he saw her blush slightly in another effort to control her giggles.

"I had to make up parts of it," she told him.

Considering Phoebe's work more closely, Ogier was reminded of the softly folded skirts Pippa wore. In Rossetti's picture the lady's head was adorned with what seemed to be a pleated scarf. In Phoebe's a thick band held back her hair. The knight knelt at his lady's feet as she tied the pennant to his vertical spear. Phoebe had attempted to capture the absorbed expression on the lady's face. The knight's stare was directed straight into the face of his mistress.

"Be sure to put that in your folder," Ogier said matter-of-factly. "It's good. You may be glad to have kept your art work in years to come. Well, I'll be off to the castle then, Alison, to collect your young man." He made his way to Penwhapple to see Sylvia.

The old tower house stood on a promontory, on either side of which the ground fell steeply to a stream. At the prow the streams merged and proceeded amicably as one, through a picturesque ravine. Ogier approached from this direction, using a path which, in Sholto Moffat's day, had carried him and Bryony on their meanders by the burn. In that time the outings would have been accomplished without undue risk. Now the neglected path was more perilous, loose stones one moment and rain softened mud the next. More than once Ogier's feet slid under him. A pleasant smell of damp vegetation seemed to hint at the snowdrops with which the little glen was planted. On the far bank, where it was sunny, a drift was already in bloom. Ogier grasped thin branches of saplings to ease his progress, pressing through overgrown rhododendrons and stepping over the roots of older trees. Rossetti had loved the shallow-flowing Penwhapple, with its dappling of light and shade and its bed of stones. He had walked the banks again and again, turbulent with love and self-recrimination. Further along, a cave opened above the water. Here he had composed the love poems which had begun his self-destruction, the love poems to his friend's wife. Nearby lay the deep pool where he had come within a breath of committing suicide. A timber bridge crossed the first burn at a point just above the confluence. The recollection of Phoebe's straightforward version of Before the Battle flashed vividly on Ogier's imagination. He held it there, relishing its force and optimism.

A shout almost had him in the stream. Dashing between the birch trees came Antony, his frame seeming to crackle with electricity, his feet snapping along the path. "Mr Boyd! Mr Boyd! I've been fishing!" He began tugging at Ogier's hand.

Ogier obligingly followed. "I hope you haven't been playing near the pool," he said. The child scrambled on ahead, sure-footed and brisk, weaving through the skeletons of bramble and stumps of decayed fern. When they came to the pool he at once leapt on a semi-circle of rock at its edge. Ogier quietly held him back. "Steady on, Antony. You'd find it a very cold bath."

Excitedly Antony shook him off. "Look, there's a fish! Can you see? And another!"

Ogier believed there might have been something tiny fleeing across the depths into which Rossetti had stared with such pain. A gentle rustling in the birch saplings suggested the stirring of the joy he must also have experienced. "Does Miss Moffat know you're here on your own?"

Antony shrugged. "Probably."

"Shall we go back now, to see what she is doing?" They walked at a slower pace along the burn. "This used to be painted dark green," Ogier remarked, when they came to the wooden bridge.

"I'll paint it for Aunt Sylvia. She'll be so pleased."

"I wonder. What will not please her is your running down here without telling her. It must never happen again. I want your solemn promise, please."

No promise was given, but a slight shrug indicated that Ogier's rebuke had taken effect. They climbed the last steep ascent, panting and in silence. As they neared the top a car could be heard, slowing a little when it came to the gates.

Sylvia was lying along the horse-hair daybed in the library, bolstered with tapestry cushions. "Don't go away," she called. "I've had such an enjoyable afternoon." She pummelled the cushions into the small of her back and struggled into a more upright position.

Ogier and Antony fell into the armchairs. "We never went to the cave," Antony informed her tragically.

"I hope you weren't worried about him?" Ogier asked.

"Not at all."

"He got as far as the pool, quite unsupervised. We have very strict rules about that area, you know."

"I think some tea would be nice. Has Ant told you? He and I have opened the summer parlour, so we can enjoy those magical views." She made no move towards making tea, but smiled lovingly from Ogier to the small boy, holding out an arm to him. Antony ran over and hugged her. "Forgive me for saying this, dear Ogier. It seems such a shame that you of all people should not have a family of your own. There, I've not offended you, I hope."

"Of course not! When, if not in the Spring, is it permissible to say such things? Was that a car I heard driving away?"

Sylvia passed a hand through Antony's hair. They exchanged mutually satisfied regards of the kind which so irritated Iona. Ogier smiled, fancying that Sylvia was not going to reply. Then she said, "Oh, the car. Yes, it was Mr Hogarth, Antony's Daddy! Just think, Childe. He had come from seeing your Mummy, and was so sorry not to find you!"

"Hal Hogarth. I was thinking about Hal only this afternoon, strangely enough. The bicycle workshops have gone steadily downhill since he left us." Ogier caught Sylvia's eye and glanced quickly towards Antony. "You do realise the situation, don't you?" The child's apparent lack of concern worried Ogier.

"What colour? What colour shall we paint the bridge? Antony demanded. "Mr Boyd wants it green. Will you show me pictures of people on it long ago?"

People long ago, thought Ogier. Through the window he glimpsed the springtime cloudscape. What was the point of nurturing vain longings? Recollecting himself, Ogier took an envelope from his inside pocket, saying, "I'll leave the budget projections on the table, shall I? Please look at the salary line in particular. Not easy, I'm afraid. Getting the VAT rebate will help but is only a one-off."

"Drummond will take us through the figures, I'm sure."

If Ogier wanted to say more, he thought better of it. Carefully placing the envelope on the library table, he said, "I'll leave the papers here then."

Iona telephoned some time after Ogier and Antony had left. "Don't forget I've got that smoked salmon. You did want it, didn't you?"

"Yes of course. Many thanks. How much do I owe you?"

"Oh, the usual. Five pounds twenty. By the way, was that Antony's father you were entertaining at the castle this afternoon?"

"I'll fetch the salmon tomorrow."

"Yes, do. I'll give you lunch. If it was Hal Hogarth I hope you'll have as little to do with him as possible. He mustn't play you off against Antony's mother."

"Ridiculous. You're being over-dramatic, Iona. Alison Hogarth and her husband are on perfectly friendly terms."

"The fact is you have been so good to Antony. Do be realistic with the parents, for your own sake. Oh, and there's something else I wanted to mention. You know Tiffany is coming up next weekend. If Antony's at the castle I've told her she's to bring him for meals, and you with him. You've been feeding other people quite enough. I take it for granted you'll be able to come?"

Sylvia was never one to argue needlessly. Today the disinclination was overwhelming.

Chapter 5

"Penwhapple is a modest fortalice, what we call a tower house in Scotland. There's a banqueting hall attached." Lionel had decided to receive the two Canadians in Drummond's office rather than his own. According to Ricky they had pots of money, wrote cookery books and were probably lesbian. "It commands a picturesque burn, which has certain romantic associations. But it is of no interest to the general public."

"It's steeped in culture," Ricky put in. "With the Rossetti connection, and all its Pre-Raphaelite visitors."

Gloria Lance brightened. From her well-cut linen suit and sensible shoes Lionel presumed she was the butch one. Her younger companion was the more athletic. She wore a cream Arran sweater. It occurred to him that the lesbianism might be one of Ricky's fabrications. There was, in fact, something very feminine about both women.

"We just love the Pre-Raphaelites, Mr Moffat." Josephine Feinstein's soft, grey gaze was gathering in intent. "Those luscious damsels and their cute pageboys. It's the mediaeval that gets us going."

"Yes, Penwhapple is not lacking in scholarly interest. It can't boast connections with Mary Queen of Scots, which must be in its favour. And of course there's the King's Quair. A mural, rather dilapidated, but certainly well known."

"Your sister would be looking for eight hundred thousand?" Catching Lionel's expression of surprise, and mistaking its significance, Josephine added, "The contents to be negotiated separately?"

Lionel uttered an inscrutable laugh. After a pause he said, "I have to be careful what I say here. The castle is jointly owned by my two sisters, my brother and myself. My sister is very fond of it. We thought we might go for a lease rather than a sale."

"Oh, right? Well, that might suit us in the short term, what do you say, Jo?" Gloria sounded more intrepid than she looked. Her expression was anxious. She was half in love with the notion of ownership. She had almost concocted a list of visitors from Ontario.

"Sure, sure." A corresponding hesitancy seemed to touch Josephine.

Ricky asked if they had furniture in store. Lionel listened to their replies with a teasing expression. "You cannot wait to put tartan carpets on the floor," he suggested.

"Hey, steady on, Mr Moffat! That is arrant nonsense!" Josephine uttered a bark of laughter. "Carpets, he says? We'd better see the place first." And she jotted tartan carpets on another mental list, allowing Miss Feinstein to hand up her bag from the floor.

From the window Lionel watched Ricky showing the Canadians to their car. Ricky's own car was parked in Drummond's usual space. Into Lionel's consciousness there flowed a sweet complaisance. Where did the boy get that airy charm? Hair too long, lemon-coloured suede shoes with a blue suit. Slightly over the top. But the youthful effect appealed.

"How do you think it went?" Ricky asked breezily, as he came back into the room.

"No shortage of the feel-good factor. An amusing couple, if couple is the word."

"How did you like the stuff about clootie dumplings and smokies? I told you that would come up."

"It would come up if I ate it. So they write cookery books, do they?"

"They inspire people to be more creative, Dad. They're just what Penwhapple needs."

"What on earth possessed you to tell them the castle was for sale? I nearly gagged when the younger one named the price you'd given them."

"Um, well, I got sort of carried away. Sorry if it pains you, but what is the point of holding on? We can't afford to maintain the fabric properly or even catalogue the contents. Who wants the place?"

"Hang on a minute! The Moffats do. Don't disparage Penwhapple because the end of an era is signalled. Maintenance has certainly become a headache and a scholarly inventory is overdue. But Drummond has produced an annotated version of the one we prepared for the insurance company. Heroic effort, believe me. Negotiations with the Royal Museum require patience, that's all."

"Aunt Sylvia?"

"She might take to The Couple. Realise that finding suitable tenants is not out of the question. But it will have to be presented to her carefully."

Ricky smiled encouragingly at his father.

"Sit down a moment, Ricky. A couple of things I've been meaning to say. First let me tell you I shall be moving into this room permanently. You will inherit mine. Aha! That puts a gleam in your eye."

"Do I get to keep the direct line?"

"Sit down please. I know your views on the office telephone system. But first, that car of yours."

The gleam glazed a fraction.

"I was against the BMW, as you know. You were in line for a modest executive saloon. But no, you insisted a second-hand BMW would be better value. Unfortunately, even a splendid car needs to be serviced. You can't expect the firm to subsidise your private motoring as well as your image."

"The broken wing mirror was honestly not my fault."

"But you were on pleasure bent. Pay that element of the bill yourself. Impress the staff. Cut a dash morally, my dear boy. There's more to life than fast cars and trendy clothes." Lionel's eye beamed sartorial approval.

"Very well, Dad. Though quite honestly, if things are that tight we really had better think again about merging with Haggarts."

Lionel walked to the window, shaking his head. "Not wise to make overtures to Haggarts now. But the idea is there. It's maturing. By the bye" - the eyebrow lifted - "please don't ring Tiffany from the office when she's down here next month. I'm sorry to be a bore but it's staff decorum again. Your private conversations may be crucial but they are inconvenient."

"I don't ring her. She rings me. What's more, I ask her to get me on the mobile, not at the office."

Lionel widened his eyes like a prim maiden aunt. "Dear me! I can't fault your businesslike approach to romance, at any rate.

Getting interested in that friend of hers, are you? I recognise the type. As captivating as they are calculating. What did you say her name was? Pippa something?"

"Pippa Cursiter, Dad. We've had this conversation before. Father a chiropodist. Remember?"

"Of course. From Corstorphine. No need to be defensive. But you know what they say about the Edinburgh bourgeoisie?" Smirking. "All fur coat and no knickers."

"Could we lift this to a higher plane?" Ricky's dispassionate gaze matched the drawl in his voice.

"Indeed we can. Take a tip, old chap. The confidences you and Tiffany exchange are heard all over the office. Not exactly relevant to your work."

"Too right! Relevant to hers! All about working for the Minister of State, whoever he is." Ricky's heavy lidded contempt was eloquent - and it was directed at his Father. Ricky saw through Lionel's determination to control things, envy giving prurience an edge.

Towards the end of the afternoon there was a telephone call from Gwen, with news about Drummond. The doctor had had to be summoned, and there had been some question of getting him into hospital. Lionel asked if he should come round, aware that part of him hoped the answer would be yes.

"He's asleep at the moment. Certainly come tomorrow. Cheer him up. I thought you ought to know what Dr Schofield said. He couldn't give Drummond longer than three months."

"Has Drummond been told?"

"No. But he looked awful. I'm sure he must guess."

"I'll come round as soon as I can. Just for a few minutes. In fact, looking at the time, I'll come now. Get the single malt out. We can both do with a dram."

The Dower House was one of several properties which the Moffats had acquired in Ayr. Originally intended for a professional family with a large establishment, it had been divided into flats by Drummond's parents, who had taken out the original staircase. Drummond and Gwen had the upper floor, which was reached by a new staircase tacked onto the side. There was a small conservatory at its foot.

Lionel thought it an unsatisfactory arrangement. Hopeless for a dog. Valuable place though, on its big corner site. The coachman's cottage and garaging were just asking for redevelopment. Scope for institutional use, assuming planning agreement could be obtained.

That was another thing Lionel disliked: the way Drummond's collection of de Morgan lustre-ware was displayed. It was in a top-lit alcove, as if the drawing room was a municipal museum. Drooling, soft toned luminosity - as suspect, almost, as Pippa Cursiter's charm. Otherwise the room was respectable enough. Drummond's old desk was the only good piece of furniture. It was a late seventeenth century escritoire, with a drop front. There was a good Persian carpet and a chesterfield full of old copies of Country Life. The chesterfield was probably quite valuable. The desk certainly was. So, of course, was the lustre-ware.

Gwen was wearing a silk wrap-over dress and heeled little slippers. Leaking perfume, she brought a measure of whisky to her brother-in-law and gave herself a marginally larger one. Of Fogo there was no sign.

"It's the first time I've seen Drummond in such a bad way," she confided. "I'm sorry you can't look in on him, Lionel, but I really must let him rest." A circumstantial account of the afternoon's events followed. Lionel gathered that Drummond had been helping with the washing up. He savoured that. "Then he turned a ghastly grey colour and staggered to sit down."

"Where?" A literal question, but his sister-in-law had a literal mind.

"He had to steady himself against the cooker. I caught hold of him almost immediately. Somehow I got him here and onto the settee."

They fancied they heard an unhappy cry from the bedroom.

Gwen rose gracefully and hurried out. Her return was calm. "It was only the dog. I've had to shut him in the kitchen. Drummond's breathing is still dreadfully heavy." Without a pause she continued where she had left off, eventually getting to the three months prognosis. "Imagine Sylvia having an attack like that! Stuck in her unsuitable place. It was actually one of my first thoughts when Dr Schofield had gone. She's over seventy, Lionel. We're none of us getting younger."

Lionel's eyes glittered. To him, Gwen's banality was a large part of her charm. "Don't give up on your own youth, or where will we be?" She lifted a shoulder. "You look very pretty when you're annoyed," he told her.

She avoided his deliberate gaze, saying, "You haven't much sense of occasion, Lionel," and began to light a cigarette.

With a characteristic sniff, flicking his nose with his finger, he waited a moment and told her she Should Not Smoke.

"You didn't come here to be patronising, did you?"

"Gwen, people die from smoking. How can you light up, with Drummond's lungs full of cancer?"

She winced, then jabbed the life out of the cigarette. On what he read as a pretext she again left the room.

Lionel stood up, preparing for departure. He crossed to the brightly lit alcove and took down a goblet. It was one of a pair and had an iridescent, red glaze. For a moment he turned it in his hands, enjoying the fantastic birds with which it was decorated. Then he set it down and took out the largest piece in the collection, a shallow peacock dish. This one he liked less. The most valuable item was a straightforward little tumbler which had been known as the Sangrail in Bryony's time. All the pieces had once been in regular use at the school. The Sangrail suggested seawater, aquamarine enhanced with gold, weed and fish in the lower half.

Years ago Lionel had dipped into a book about Victorian ceramics. Was it Edward de Morgan who had had to be followed by someone with a chair when he visited his showrooms? The chair was placed strategically when, as regularly happened, Edward de Morgan sat down at random. Lionel returned the dish carefully to its shelf, gesturing as Gwen reappeared. "There's a collection of these ghastly objects in Birmingham, isn't there?"

"Oh yes." Gwen regarded him with a mournful expression. "It's strange you should have said that, Lionel. It was one of the happiest days of our marriage, going to see the lustre-ware in Birmingham Art Gallery."

Lionel went to embrace her. It was a brief, brotherly hug. His next inclination was to sink back into one of the chairs, not without first checking it was there. "Rather an exhausting afternoon," he told her. "Ricky brought in a couple of Canadians. He enjoyed himself, so of course they did too. They may think we got them on a false prospectus." He explained Ricky's intervention over the castle.

"It does sound rather rash of Ricky. But what a blessing it would be not to have all that worry any more."

"Precisely. Perhaps you could see these Canadians, try to mollify them. They'd love you, I mean really love you. Ricky thinks they're lesbians."

"He's becoming as cynical as his father."

Lionel stood up abruptly, closing his mind to the thought of how cynical Ricky's father was. "Get some rest. I expect tomorrow will be demanding, physically and mentally. Tell Drummond I was sorry not to speak to him, and make sure Schofield doesn't forget about the physio. Give me a call if Drummond needs bracing up, or if you want me to put a bomb under the doctor." He wondered whether he should ask Gwen to let him have Drummond's tweed suit. She could easily throw it out. The family tweed was not made now, and the suit might do for Ricky if it was cut down.

"I'll ring Iona and Sylvia. They'll have to know." Gwen went as far as the top of the stairs and watched him descend to the outer door. She wished she had confided in him more. Told him of Drummond's obsession with leaving Tiffany his old desk.

Behind her she could hear Fogo whining hopefully.

Chapter 6

The car drove past the Lodge rather too quickly, leaving a rough impression on the ground. From what Iona could make out the driver was in white overalls with a blue blouse underneath the bib. He had a head of wavy hair and was smoking. She walked up to the castle, dragged at the heavy bell pull and waited. Eventually she heard voices on the stairs.

"You haven't been up on the tower again?" she demanded, as Sylvia and Antony opened the door together.

"Of course not. We were having another look at the old mural. Ant notices all the little details, and points them out to me."

Iona allowed herself to be persuaded inside with her customary show of reluctance. "Do you really think you should be clambering up and down this draughty staircase?"

Antony shrank back dramatically against Sylvia, bringing her to a halt on the wide, carpeted landing. "I love looking at the mural," was Sylvia's matter-of-fact reply. "It's not everyone who'll do it with me."

"Just so long as you aren't being bullied. You could easily miss your footing if you're paying attention to the walls." Iona's laugh was a dry punctuation mark.

"I know when to stop." Sylvia caught Antony's eye. He gazed back with mesmeric affection. Gently, she released her arm. They went into the library. Books were lying about, some displaying their illustrations. "His reading is coming on splendidly. Ogier has promised us more books for tomorrow's session."

Antony lolled at Sylvia's knees, his eyes on Iona. "Tennyson was quite a selfish man," he told her.

"Fancy you knowing that!" Iona did not care for his triumphant expression. "But I see it all the time. One human being can be very selfish to another." She gave Antony a perfunctory smile. "Has Annie been helpful?" she went on, adjusting the perspective. More vexing than infant tyranny was a sister's rugged independence.

"Indeed she has. And so has Pat." Pat was Annie's husband; Antony had been helping him in the woodland garden that afternoon.

"Pat's helping me paint the bridge!" Antony exclaimed. He jumped down and began running round the chairs in a figure of eight. He stopped and fixed Iona again with his long-lashed eyes. "Shall I read you a story?"

"I can't stay, I'm afraid. You could fetch a book and show it to me." How Antony's presence frustrated her! "I'm rather thirsty," she lied. "Could you be clever enough to bring me a glass of water, do you think?"

He was off like a shot. Pattering feet, then silence.

"I saw that awful old car again this afternoon. That's why I came round. It was Mr Hogarth, I take it? I do so hope he isn't unsettling the little boy. Even more important, as far as I am concerned, unsettling you."

"Not in the least. It's only his second visit, perhaps his third. I find him rather fun, as a matter of fact."

"So you're entertaining him as well as his son?"

"No. I don't entertain him! He and Ant spent most of their time in the kitchen with Annie, as it happens. Oh, there was something else! He wanted to sell me his car!"

"That old Jaguar?"

"Yes, I think that must be the one. I find him very engaging. Casual but most polite."

"Well, please bear in mind that all is not well between him and Antony's mother, as you claimed it was, and please don't let yourself become too involved. I hope you won't regret having Antony up here in the afternoons. Your kind heart runs away with you."

"Nonsense. I usually suit myself entirely." Sylvia's serene smile faded. "Poor Ant. We really have cheered each other up, you know." Just as suddenly the smile returned. She said, "Mr Hogarth is full of surprises."

The sun shone through the solar, giving immediacy to Sholto's corbies in the recess. In the indirect light Iona's hair had an iridescent sheen. Antony burst back into the room. With as much grace as she could muster, Iona received a slopping glass of tepid water. Sylvia reflected sadly that she could not for ever resist family pressure to be rescued from the little boy. "Chance is a fine thing," she announced.

"Well, Childe, time to get back to Somersby and find your mother."

"I wish you'd let me take over for a bit," said Iona, as they made their way down the stairs. She accepted a lift, although it would have been quicker to walk. She waved as Sylvia swung out into the narrow lane, hitting the kerb.

"You hit that kerb too," Antony pointed out when, a hundred yards further on, they turned into the school grounds.

"I don't think so."

As they drew up at Somersby Antony became excited. He jumped out as soon as they stopped and dashed off, leaving his door open. An uncharacteristic peace reigned. Sylvia could hear him calling his mother. She went round to the art room, as though guided by some etheric hand.

The local newspaper lay open on the big trestle table . "Laird to Sell," she read. The story was about Penwhapple, and did not bear out the headline.

Earlier that afternoon Pippa had become embroiled in yet another incident at the tree house. A group of juniors had piled brushwood round the trunk and were poised to set it alight. Pippa demanded and got the matches from the ground party. Taunts and jeers came from above. She knew who was there. With her free hand she began tearing away the banks of kindling. The mildest of the boys tried to snatch the matches back.

Pippa swung away, still eyeing him, and he clouted her on the nose. The intention had been to shock the matches from her grasp. Pippa felt the bridge was not necessarily broken, but the pain was blinding. She dropped the matchbox and nursed her nose with both hands, involuntary tears running over them.

"I'm sorry, Miss Cursiter. I'm really sorry! I honestly didn't mean to hit you!"

The matches were retrieved and proffered once more. Pippa received them, now dabbing for blood with a hanky. "Go to your rooms, all of you, and stay there." She glanced up. "Right. You can come down."

"You can come up!"

"Robert! Come down at once. I'm minded to send you to Mr Boyd."

The pain in her nose made it feel ten sizes too large. The idea of her ugliness gave her strength. Robert descended. Pippa dispatched him, too, to his room, then retired to the Cottage. She bathed her nose, pressing it from side to side. She scrubbed her face in cold water. Then she brushed her hair, pushing it through a severe, black band. She applied a touch of eau de toilette behind her ears, studying herself in the mirror gravely. Her skin was faintly pink over the cheeks. Her nose looked normal.

Slowly she climbed the front steps of the Mansion. There was a stain of apricot in the late afternoon sky. She drew strength from its reflection.

The midges were beginning to bite. It was possible she had been seen from the staff room. She moved indoors. It was chill and dark after the warmth outside.

Through the door she glimpsed the capstan table. It was here she had raised the question of pets, with unsatisfactory results. The table was designed to seat twelve, and there was an option for more space as the top was cranked round. Ogier had nice hands. The room was faded, functional, haunted by hard-fought controversies. She moved up the stairs, gingerly touching the end of her nose. It was still sore. With a psychological effort she made the pain worse.

From the tall landing window Pippa looked again at the declining sun, the apricot flush changing to delicate saffron. The outer office was empty. She knocked on the inner door and opened it, not sure if Ogier had responded. He was there, sprawled in his old, work-worn chair, the stuffing sprouting from its gashed leather. She closed the door behind her, saying, "I'd like a word, if you're not too busy."

He rose, gesturing her to a chair. Her impression of him was, as usual, mixed. His hair was too scant. She disliked the colour. It was a faded version of her own. Dark hair would have been better. His thin legs were clad in rough wool socks. He resumed his seat, first laying a book on his desk. His kilt had retreated into subtler blues, greens and lovats than those of the original hunting tartan. It was the one he usually wore, so old it was beginning to look disreputable.

Pippa settled, making herself wait until she had composed her thoughts. She explained what had taken place at the tree house. As Ogier opened and extended the palm of one hand it struck her that his fingers were oddly shaped. Not nice after all. But she could not help warming to the fair little hairs on the backs, and over his wrists.

He was pleasantly sunburnt, and the hairs were bleached.

"Show me where you were hit." Ogier leaned forward, amazed that anyone should dream of touching this self-assured girl. His bony knees were wide apart. Pippa's eyes were drawn into the dark recess between.

"Here." Her fingers poignantly revolved around the injured spot.

"Painful?"

"Very."

"But not broken?" Their eyes met above her stilled hand. His concern engaged her most friendly feelings.

"I don't suppose it's broken." Those muffled tones sounded a feminine appeal.

Ogier extended one of his odd-shaped fingers, then thought better of it. "Well, I'm sorry. I'll speak to Robert. As you say, it's not the first time he's made a nuisance of himself at the tree house." The feeling of intimacy was maintained. "Why don't you get Samantha to put something on your . . ." He chose "face" rather than "nose," fearing the latter might have comic connotations. "I'm only sorry it had to be Robert again."

"I know you think I single him out for criticism. It's just that I find he has limited intelligence."

Ogier, instead of replying, stood up. Pippa slowly stood up beside him. I can't remember seeing her smile, he thought.

At that moment her face lit. "Does it look hideous?" she asked.

He went to open the door for her. In that instant his dwindling hair, stooped figure, the battle-scarred kilt, his unsatisfactory hands, the courteous gesture, all caused her to react. Nothing happened externally. But within she felt liberated.

"I'm not joking," she said. "I want to know if it looks hideous." She could hardly breath. Her lungs needed air, her heart was starved of blood. "Please, Ogier."

Still he held the door ajar, waiting.

"I said, my nose hurts. It may look awful tomorrow. Help me."

Ogier put his hands on her shoulders. "That better?" he asked. The pressure of his hands was firm, his voice serious.

She gave him a smile that positively illuminated him. "Infinitely better."

"Now, from physician to judge. I must find Robert rapidly, while the incident is still fresh in everyone's mind. Meanwhile, do see Samantha."

As they returned to the door they heard the sound of noisy weeping in the hallway downstairs. Ogier paused. Pippa put her softly clad arms over his shoulders. As he withdrew slightly she pressed on his chest, her chin raised, her eyes fixed on his. Feeling the pressure of her plump breasts, his heart laboured painfully. He moved away again.

"Dear Ogier." She gave him another, more hesitant smile.

As he kissed her mouth her arms went limp. His tightened. The intense intimacy of her lips, not passive but in motion, expressed poignant sexuality. He returned the pressure, tasting her mouth, yielding to the illusion of possessing her body. Her face withdrew. The voices were nearer now. As Ogier and Pippa drew further apart Antony rushed in, followed by Samantha and, less closely, by Sylvia. A distressed look crossed Sylvia's face.

"I want Mummy," Antony told them. But Mummy was not there. She was with her husband, trying to sort out their unsatisfactory marriage.

"Good heavens," exclaimed Iona, as she opened her front door. Her surprise was caused not by finding her sister on the doorstep but by seeing Antony in the car. "Do my eyes deceive me, or is that the Childe directing operations from the back seat?"

"They do not deceive you. I have him for the simple reason his mother was not there. There are extenuating circumstances."

"There always are. Won't you come in for a while?"

"I won't stay. We had a bit of a weep down at the school. I think he's in need of a story and an early night." Sylvia glanced back at the car. "There was just one matter I have on my mind."

Iona waited. She disliked standing, and never chose to do so at her own front door.

Sylvia said, "I may sound like an old clapperdin. But I am very worried."

Again Iona found herself waiting. She attempted to reassure and prompt her sister, imagining it must be Drummond's cancer that was the worry. "I know, dear. But we must be as positive as we can. That is the best way we can help him now. We must be positive for Gwen's sake too."

Antony began knocking on the car window. Then he rolled it down and stuck his head through. He resumed his knocking on the side of the car. Every so often he expressed a loud, shuddering sniff.

"Not Drummond. Ogier. I had one of my clear-sighted episodes this afternoon. You know how I hate them. I began to be aware of it as I followed Ant towards the school. His mother was not there, as I've told you, but we found Ogier in the office. That was later. I knew it as if he had confessed to me."

"A confession?" Iona inquired, again gently, and after a pause.

"There was no disguising it. To all intents and purposes he was the dear, phlegmatic man we all know. He was with the new teacher, Pippa Cursiter. But there is something deeply unprofessional about their relationship."

Iona felt an immense sense of relief. To stop herself laughing she called, "Be patient a little longer, Antony! Aunt Sylvia won't be long now." She looked at her sister and told her, with a smile, "Ogier won't lose his head over someone of Tiffany's age! You're the one who causes me unease, Sylvia. I wish you had time to come in and relax. Would it be so reprehensible if Ogier developed a Platonic affection for Pippa? She's quite attractive, and he can be so cerebral."

"I must get the Childe away. I'm glad you mentioned Tiffany. She must see Drummond when she's back this time. Promise me she'll go."

Antony had become still. He could hear the elderly ladies' solemn exchange. On an inspiration he called out, "Please come, Aunt Sylvia, or the bell might start calling you!"

The sisters stopped talking. A great silence pervaded the policies right up to the castle.

"Very well," said Iona. "I give you that promise on Tiffany's behalf. In return, I want a promise from you. You are not to let Antony cajole you up the tower. Remember how breathless those stairs make you."

Chapter 7

Gwen was already in her coat when Tiffany arrived at the Dower House.

"Come and see him. He's a little chirpier today. But don't let him talk too much. I'll have to go out at once or I'll be late."

Having welcomed Tiffany robustly at the front door, Fogo took advantage of her presence to make his cheerful way into the bedroom. Along the bottom of the bedspread his coat had left a greasy stain. "He's not allowed in here," said Gwen, observing Tiffany's amused glance. "I think I'll just shut him away."

Tiffany's good humour vanished when she looked more closely at her Uncle. This was not the Uncle Drummond who had always put himself out to amuse and oblige her. He used to have such a solid head and full, broad face. Now even the bone structure seemed diminished. His eyes were deep with suffering behind the smile. His square shoulders were like a crudely carved, wooden coat hanger. His hand summoned her closer. Tiffany bent over and kissed his waxy forehead. She felt ill at ease in her young, healthy body.

He whispered, "Sit down." His voice came raspingly.

Tiffany obeyed, wondering at such masterful intent from such a forlorn situation.

"I've arranged for Haggart to come here at half past eleven. I shall want you to get me through to the sitting room. You won't need to say anything. Just listen." Between sentences the breath came in pants. "I've also asked the people from downstairs to come at twenty to twelve. I shall want you to let them in."

Tiffany agreed, with such a heightened sense of unreality that she feared she might fail in these simple tasks. They heard Gwen leaving by the conservatory. While he was still capable of light exertion Drummond had filled it with geraniums. The lower door closed. A conspiratorial silence fell. "Open the window," Drummond muttered, a half-humorous pout indicating it was against the rules.

The room was stiflingly warm. Drummond was watching her with such gentle eyes that Tiffany was prompted to take one of his hands between hers. The moment was tense. She knelt quickly on the carpet at his side. To cover her awkwardness she launched into an account of developments in her job. She had just been promoted, and would be moving to London. "No-one thought Lord Venables would let a woman have the job. He likes me because I'm from Ayrshire. As Minister of State he covers the complete range of policy. It will be fantastic experience."

"North Ayrshire, isn't he? We're South, remember."

"Yes, Uncle Drummond, but I got the job."

"Still singing in your choir, are you?"

"Definitely! They say Edinburgh's cliquey but I've never noticed it. We have all sorts, it's so friendly. I think I shall miss the choir more than anything else when I move."

Drummond heard her out. Then he said, "Now, can you help me into the wheelchair?"

Not without difficulty, and a great deal of anxiety, Tiffany guided him off the bed and into the chair, supported with cushions. She covered his knees with a light rug. Then, according to his instructions, she propelled him into the sitting room.

The doorbell rang so promptly it startled them. Tiffany hurried down to admit the family solicitor. She was moved by George Haggart's affection for her Uncle. She sat a little away from the two men, with a mixture of curiosity and dread.

Haggart pulled his chair nearer to Drummond, who exuded an almost excited courtesy of his own. Still haltingly, and barely audibly, he embarked on a recitation of his feelings for his sister Iona. He had never had children of his own and regarded Tiffany as a daughter. He wanted to leave Tiffany something personal in his will. It was an omission that bothered him greatly. Something substantial, like the de Morgan lustre-ware. He also wanted her to have his desk. "But everything else to my wife. Nothing to harm her interests."

Labouring to express all that was on his mind, and encouraged by Haggart's friendly attention, Drummond at last fell silent. It had been harrowing listening to him, so weak were his condition and his voice. Tiffany sat in her armchair, distressed, humbled and elated in equal measure. She attempted to speak, but Drummond raised a steady hand. "Can you draw up a document to that effect? And will it be legally binding?"

The solicitor readily reassured him, glancing round the room for paper on which to commit his client's wishes. Tiffany watched him light upon a piece of blue paper protruding from a shelf. He took it up, with a leather folder for the Radio Times. Writing on his knees he made out the document. There was just enough time to read it through before the bell rang again. Tiffany went to let in the couple from downstairs. They found Drummond limp with exhaustion. He signalled to Tiffany to go out and make coffee for them all.

She was glad to escape. She supposed the codicil was being signed. Fogo greeted her with delight, frisking about and snatching up his spongy rubber ball. With short legs for the length of his body, he lacked speed and agility. Tiffany tossed the ball and he went skidding over the linoleum. Floundering back, he demanded a greater challenge than the kitchen could supply. Tiffany waited for the kettle to boil. To have seen Drummond's eloquent struggle had been terrible. She wouldn't have wanted him to endure such stress for any desk or lustreware, however valuable.

She found some chocolate ginger nuts and tumbled them into a bowl. She made five coffees, then realised that Drummond would not want any. Every item in Gwen's fridge seemed to be wrapped, labelled and dated.

She fancied her reappearance caused an uneasy stir. A few remarks were addressed to her but it was uncanny how hypocritical she had started to feel. She sensed that they all, even George Haggart, viewed her as a manipulator. Fogo preceded her into the room, making straight for Drummond and leaping onto his lap.

"He's all right." Drummond fondled the dog's rough-haired head. Again he made his comically pouting mouth.

When the visitors had gone Tiffany set herself to distract her uncle by resuming the account of work in Edinburgh. But he signalled curtly that she should wash the dirty cups. Tiffany understood. The evidence had to be removed. He asked her to help him back to bed. Fogo, he insisted, should remain with him. It was another hour before Gwen arrived. By then Drummond was asleep. Tiffany slipped into the sitting room to meet her.

"I bumped into Ricky." Gwen told her. " We had coffee. Lionel wants me to meet some Canadian clients. Now I think of it, Ricky never noticed my new hairdo."

"It looks super."

Gwen smiled sweetly. "Unless I'm much mistaken, I believe Ricky's rather fond of you. Affection between cousins often develops into something more special. I'm very fond of Ricky and I flatter myself I understand him better than most people. That includes his father by the way. He hasn't had an easy upbringing, has he, seeing his mother on that formal basis, and with Lionel inclined to expect so much. Now, how's the patient behaved himself?"

"He fell asleep about half an hour ago. We had a long talk. Then his voice got tired. I offered to read and he seemed to like that."

"Oh? And what did you read?"

"Actually it was a book I brought in case he fell asleep. I began again at the beginning."

Gwen began to potter about the room, looking into drawers and along bookshelves. "Where did I put that thing?" she murmured. "I could swear it was here last night."

"What?" asked Tiffany in an indifferent voice, her thoughts straying to Ricky.

"The print-out of a memorial service Drummond attended last year. I wanted to refer to it."

Tiffany felt herself grow cold. Gwen could only be anticipating Drummond's death. Was it admirable to be thinking of the practical aspects of his funeral at this time, or was it chillingly premature?

"I had it yesterday. Just a sheet of blue paper."

Tiffany's metabolism seemed to falter. A bad dream had become reality. She kept silent. Yet she had to speak! She had at least to convey something to Gwen of what her uncle had done. Not the means. Those details could wait. Just the end. The less said the better, especially by herself. It would all be common knowledge soon. But Gwen must not be needlessly hurt. She declared suddenly, and rather diffidently, "There's something Uncle Drummond said recently which I expect you know about. He wants me to have his desk." She could not bring herself to mention the lustre-ware. She added, "And one or two other things." Her voice dwindled into a silence.

Gwen's search came to an end. She stood beside the desk in

question, papers that were not blue in her hand. "I know all about the desk," she said, opening it, placing her papers carefully inside and closing it again. Tiffany's words were stored with equal care. It seemed to Tiffany that her fatal message had been received. Yet the atmosphere had not changed. Drummond called. She followed Gwen into the bedroom. Gwen noticed the open window and shut it. Fogo wagged his tail guardedly from the coverlet.

"You must keep warm, darling. Tiffany doesn't realise the danger of draughts. I gather she's been reading to you?"

"I feel better," Drummond asserted. "It was a peculiar book. But I enjoyed it. I enjoyed hearing Tiffany's ideas about life."

Gwen perched on the bed stroking his hand. "Do you feel like some tea? Get down, Fogo. I've greeted you once already."

Drummond was wanly shaking his head. "Nothing." There was a childish resignation in the gesture.

Gwen went on holding his hand for a while, and Fogo continued to thrust his nose into her lap. "Come on," she said. "I must get you some lunch. Tiffany must be off. And I am going to put this dog out of here once and for all. Tiffany, dear, I did tell you Ricky sent his love, didn't I?"

As Tiffany left the Dower House the image of blue paper still floated before her. Try as she might, she could not reconstruct the part she had played that morning so that it reflected more creditably on herself.

After she had gone, Gwen stood alone in the sitting room. One by one she considered the collection of de Morgan pots. Her eyes lingered on the Sangrail, the most valuable of them all.

Tiffany had been lying. The desk indeed. The desk was a silly obsession of Drummond's, a way of trying to explain something else. If he intended to execute one of the famous Moffat trusts in his niece's benefit, she would fight it. She would need every penny she could get if she was to be left on her own. Perhaps she would see those Canadians Ricky had told her about.

She snatched up the Sangrail and held it as though poised to crush it. She could open a window and hurl it out. She could dash it on the kitchen floor. But she did nothing of the sort with so precious an object. She simply hid it in the top shelf of the linen cupboard. Then she came back to the silent sitting room and lit a cigarette.

Fogo was whining in the kitchen. She ignored him. There would be time for Fogo when she had finished her cigarette and was getting Drummond's lunch.

Chapter 8

The sun lay like a skin over the water, masking its sullenness with a superficial smile. As they drew nearer the brightness withdrew. Ricky, settling on the grass, tossed the hair out of his eyes, saying "I can tell you one thing. I'd require a seriously hefty bribe to swim in that crocodile pool."

Tiffany smiled enigmatically. Pippa seemed not to have heard. What was a classy bird like this doing in rural Ayrshire, Ricky asked himself, the land which time forgot? One day he might try the Moffat charm on her.

Tiffany chose her own place to sit. She drew up her knees and hunched her shoulders in an expression of pleasure. Midsummer at Penwhapple. A walk across the hills to watch the sunrise. And then, for her, London. "Only one patch of blue in sight," she informed them, scrutinising the sample of sky above the tree-fringed water. "I'm glad you're seeing the pool all murky, Pip."

Ricky watched Pippa as she stood at the edge of the pool, staring at her own reflection. The surface creased with a light gust of wind. "Don't you wish Rossetti had drowned himself?" he said. "Put another fifty thousand onto the castle, easily."

"It's more subtle that he didn't," said Tiffany.

Pippa drew in her breath. Turning away from the pool, she rearranged her full skirt of Indian cotton and removed her sandals, aware that Ricky was watching her.

"Come on, Ricky," said Tiffany. "Tell us who these Canadians are."

"My dear cousin, doesn't your mother tell you anything?"

"Oh, everything that has been carefully sanitised. I gather we've heard from the Museums Man at last."

"Ah ha!"

"And they like the idea but there's some kind of snag."

"I'll say there is. Money."

"That is where Mother's information becomes a little vague."

"It's more than vague, dear girl, it's a total blank. There is no money. The whole scheme is a non-starter."

"That's not what Mother said."

"She wouldn't, would she? Our seniors just love the Museums Man, as you call him. The Museums Man will graciously pay us peanuts for the Rossetti, the one thing he's been told he can't have. He'll maybe accept the rest if we give it all to him for nothing. Oh, I can't be bothered to talk about it."

"But surely, we'd be relieved of all the worry of conservation, insurance and cataloguing. Isn't that the point? And isn't there something about the King's Quair? They'd restore it for us?"

"Yes, provided we paid! I'll tell you something. Stewart Urquhart reckons their conservators are useless. Your Museums Man, my dear Coz, has been seriously disobliging."

The sun came out. Pippa settled herself on the grass, smoothing her skirt, her forehead creased with a small, preoccupied frown.

"And these Canadians? Where do they come in?"

"They have sporting instincts. They'd turn Penwhapple into a Theme Park." Seeing Tiffany's expression of dismay, Ricky hooted. His cousin was still the same lovable clown, rising to every tease. "I can see why Lord Venables finds you such fun. Does he explain the Enterprise Culture to you in the back of the official car?" He hooted again, aware of a perverse satisfaction in the idea of Penwhapple as a theme park. Pippa glanced at his sprawling figure. He squirmed round and put his head on her lap, murmuring something unintelligible, eyes closed.

"I hope you're comfortable," said Pippa distantly. There was, Ricky decided, something dodgy about this girl. To lay her just once might be a good plan. Pippa looked across him to Tiffany. "Have you seen Antony yet?" she said, as if Ricky wasn't there.

"Yes, that's another thing,' said Ricky, sitting up abruptly. "Antony. Rumour has it that Antony, as he is called, is killing off a very dear Maiden Aunt of mine. What am I to make of these rumours?" Abruptly he lay down again. "I await your answer."

"He's an exceptionally lucky little boy, that's all." Tiffany tried not to react to Ricky's familiarity with Pippa. "Penwhapple without the Childe, as Mum and Sylvia call him, would be Penwhapple without its spell these days."

"He'll be starting Class One in the autumn. I hope he goes right through the school, don't you Tiffany?" Pippa glanced down at Ricky's lank black hair. To Tiffany it seemed she was lifting it, strand by strand, and letting it fall back, loosely, on his forehead.

Without warning Ricky sat up again. "Do you two realise how much valuable time you've tempted me to waste?"

Pippa turned her head sideways and caught Tiffany's eye.

Ricky jumped to his feet. It was ridiculous of his aunt to be so difficult about showing the Canadians over Penwhapple. She had nothing better to do. He pulled on his jacket, saying he really must show up at the office for an hour or two.

Pippa coolly surveyed him, not bothering to move. Tiffany clambered to her feet and brushed traces of grass from his back. He set off briskly, waving as he went, without looking round. "Well," said Tiffany. "Very interesting. What has been going on this long, hot summer?"

Pippa tried hard to look displeased. "Nothing has been going on"

"I bet the BMW has been parked outside the school every night."

"It most certainly has not."

"I bet it soon will be."

"I do not like juveniles. Tell me more about your Uncle Drummond. Why does he have the Sangrail?"

There was a guarded pause. "I think it was my grandfather who retrieved it from the school, when they all realised how valuable it was. Along with the other de Morgan stuff. Why do you ask?"

"Exactly how valuable is it though?"

"I don't know. Very valuable. It's a museum piece, and so are all the others. Amazing to think of them in use at the school in Bryony's day."

"We had that strange little ritual for the leavers yesterday evening."

"Oh yes, King Arthur's knights, pledging themselves to seek the Holy Grail." The colour had mounted to Tiffany's cheeks.

Pippa said, rather deliberately, "There is something faintly comic about that ceremony. One thinks of young ladies on bicycles, setting out to change the world – complete with their typewriters."

"And they did, too! – change the world, I mean. They were not little conformists."

"I'd like to hear what you decided your Holy Grail was to be?"

"The World Service of the BBC! Oh dear, I had no idea what it was, except it was in London, and sounded good." Tiffany stole a hasty look at Pippa's face, fearing that her friend might be contemptuous of her enthusiasms, then deciding, no, Pippa was not one to be flippant. "Take this with a pinch of salt, won't you? I've had a sort of Grail experience again just recently." Somewhat gauche in manner, her voice hesitant, Tiffany went on, "I thought I might find myself struggling with this new job. Actually I love it. I enjoy making new contacts. I don't find the ringing round a bore, as I expected. The media people are generally very helpful. They have a job to do. I get a kick out of trotting about, trying to help them."

"And you get on well with Lord Venables."

"Yes. Ricky's so rude about him! I admire him. He makes up his mind. He's not brilliant on TV, his voice goes a bit high, but off-duty he can be very friendly. Everyone likes him, except the fishing industry. Uncle Drummond was funny about him. Pretended to dislike him for coming from North Ayrshire!" Tiffany stopped herself abruptly.

After a short silence Pippa said, "I'm glad. I was thinking that Ogier often talks about evil being drawn to things that are intrinsically good. He's rather fond of paradoxes. Especially gloomy ones."

Tiffany plucked at the grass. Deciding to satisfy a little curiosity of her own, she said, "Pippa, you're not getting attached to Ogier, are you?"

Pippa took time to reply. "I suppose I might be."

"Physically? He's a lot older than you. Do you find him attractive?" She could sense Pippa's defences stir. "I mean, how does he compare with a certain research fellow from our university days?"

"I can't compare him and Ogier. I hate to remember that other business now." Pippa spoke with conviction. She found herself making a fresh comparison: with Ricky. The animal immediacy, the selfishness. "I don't know," she said. "I find Ogier difficult to understand, and sometimes frustrating. The whole ethos of Somersby is so intense, so endlessly child-centred. It encourages the children to feel too important. We work hard enough all day, and then we have long staff meetings. The Wednesday meetings last for hours, 'holding the children in our consciousness,' in that rather overworked phrase. No wonder Ogier looks like a ghost half the time."

"I know what you mean. And so high minded. At the risk of being curious, I expect that could be part of the attraction?"

"It is not," Pippa said gruffly. Then her face softened. "But I do like the idea of the round table. The fact that Ogier is Chairman as much as Headmaster gives him more authority, not less. It gives the school strength. When I was doing my in-service training we had a change of headmaster. The school ethos collapsed in bickering overnight."

"Come on," said Tiffany. "I'm going to have that swim." She went closer to the pool. As she splashed the water with her hand, the surface became dappled with refracted light. Where the Penwhapple burn ran into the pool its weaving impulse shone and glittered. Where it entered the deep circle it grew shadowed and still. Tiffany started peeling off her clothes. As she removed the last vestige of clothing, a flood of sunshine appeared, casting her in golden light. The rocks at her feet, the surface of the stream, all was golden. She tied her hair in a scarf, saying, "I wish you'd come in too, Pippa."

"I agree with Ricky. No sane mortal would enter that pool without a bribe."

Tiffany stood, tall and a little awkward, half covering her small breasts with her arms. What Pippa saw was not her friend's virginity, which had threatened to become notorious in their student days, but something more austere, her chastity. Tiffany lowered herself cautiously into the water. "It's gorgeous," she exclaimed, through chattering teeth. She struck off for the far side in a choppy crawl. Trees rooted in the bank cast moving shadows. She turned and swam into the sun.

Pippa climbed to her feet and sauntered over to watch.

Tiffany started away to the far bank, once more where the water was deepest. For a moment she hung onto a muscular root above her head. The weather changed again. She launched herself back and, this time, pulled herself out as soon as she reached the rocks. Clouds had rolled up as if from nowhere, filling their private patch of sky. Tiffany stood dripping on her rock, a thin white figure, now slightly bowed. The water had become hostile and black. She dried herself and struggled into her clothes, dragging the scarf off her hair. Pippa offered her cardigan, affectionately amused. She could not take her eyes from her friend.

They made their way along the burn, following the path through the trees, Tiffany shivering in the borrowed cardigan. The water spilled over hidden obstacles, bubbling and bursting, white in its hectic progress. They crossed the confluence of streams on Antony's newly painted bridge. For a moment they lingered, a breeze blowing Pippa's skirt against the fretwork. Pippa laid a hand on the rail. She caught Tiffany's eye. They went on.

Chapter 9

Sylvia waited until Tiffany had gone back to Edinburgh and then took Antony up on the tower.

He circled the low parapet in little rushes. Strange lights glided across Sylvia's vision. She moved towards Antony with a cautionary hand. At once he leant over the parapet, easing himself forward on his stomach. The bell house on its buttress was a long way below. "I'm looking for the fairy rock," Sylvia said artfully. "Can you see it, and point it out to me?"

Antony extended an arm. Sylvia secured his hand and gazed towards Ailsa Craig. The coastline was indistinct, obscured now by low-hanging vapour, now seeming to rise like the spectre of some time-forgotten kingdom, limpid and shimmering. Sylvia's heartbeat returned to something like normality. "Do you see that bright patch of sunshine on the coast?' she murmured. "That is where King Robert the Bruce landed, to free Scotland from the Covetous King." She was still out of breath from the stairs.

"I see it," Antony assured her.

Perhaps, with the eye of innocence, he could indeed share with Sylvia that mysterious, inner landscape. She had a faint sense of the tower revolving, of Ailsa Craig as the Fortunate Isle, of Robert the Bruce's victory over the English as the fulfilment of ancient prophecy.

"We all have a Covetous King inside us, Childe Antony. We must fight that enemy, the enemy within. Only then can we fight the Covetous King in others, as Good King Robert did."

"Is this where Merlin did the picture?"

Sylvia took stock. "There. That is where Rossetti painted his picture. Sholto and Bryony, the great flag billowing behind them, little dog Fogo at their feet."

"I'm the little dog." Antony began trotting over the lead roof on his hands and knees. He sniffed Sylvia's shoes. "I'm little Fogo."

"Come on, we'll go down," she said briskly. "I've done what I promised not to. I've taken you on the roof."

"You never promised!"

"Your Auntie Iona thinks I did."

Antony ran back for another bold look over the parapet. "Goodbye, little bellhouse!"

Sylvia got him to the steps somehow. He was making his way intrepidly down in an instant, despite her injunctions to take care. Laboriously she followed, shutting the awkward door with a clap and, after a struggle, getting the bolt to slide home. The steps were so narrow she scraped the walls, sudden gloom adding to her claustrophobia. She hoped Antony would leave the lower door open. She waited a moment, breathing hard. He had vanished by the time she emerged on the landing. She closed the lower door and heard voices. He was calling her. She went down the shallow scale-and-platt stair to the head of the turnpike.

Iona was coming up. Sylvia decided to give in gracefully. This last, brief glimpse of felicity would have to do.

Chapter 10

They all trooped into the banqueting hall, Fogo running ahead. "You sit there, Lionel," said Sylvia. "It's your meeting."

Lionel took Drummond's usual chair, with a self-importance he contrived to make ironic. Iona took the chair on his right, her back to the tall windows. Gwen walked to a place opposite her. She left the chair beside Lionel vacant. Fogo trotted energetically into all corners of the room, sniffing the oak dresser and darting across the fireplace. He ignored Gwen's command to settle. Sylvia was still moving about vaguely. Then, as if by an effort of will, she lowered herself into the chair by her brother.

"We should really have Sholto's capstan table back here for this kind of meeting," Lionel told her, with sly pomposity. "More democratic. But I realise the purpose of this gathering upsets you. So I'll proceed, if everyone agrees."

He glanced round. Gwen had subdued the dog. Iona was waiting with a business-like expression. Sylvia looked vaguer than ever. Lionel gave her a quick smile. She did not respond. There was no sunshine to flood through the windows which gave the hall its splendid light. Time-honoured originality and fertility seemed to be conspicuously absent and, in their place, a sense of reckoning.

"I wanted us to meet because we seem to be losing impetus. Drummond and I had come to feel that we cannot expect the rising generation to take on Penwhapple as it is now. That would surely be the height of folly. Hence the approach we have made, with everyone's full approval, to the Royal Museum. Drummond's concept is for a Trust to be established. It would be based on the principle that the castle paid for its existence. That would mean getting it leased for perhaps five years, with an option to renew. It would be a full repairing lease, the sort of thing Ricky's Canadians might find attractive. We would get a better feel for that if we let Miss Feinstein and Miss Lance have a look at the place. Whoever takes the castle must be prepared to have it with responsibility for the contents."

"That fills me with apprehension straight away," said Sylvia.

"Well, wait a minute." Lionel pushed a heavy oak candlestick an inch further from him. "What this means, in terms of securing a lease, is that we must spend a fair amount of money on security. Also on general modernising. Putting in decent bathrooms and a modern kitchen. Repairing the fabric of the tower. Now, what is your view there, Iona?"

Iona spoke after a slight pause. "I have to admit that Penwhapple has worried me lately. I do feel it's too much for you, Sylvia. Even with Annie's loyal help. I love the place as much as anyone. But one has to be practical. It's old-fashioned and it's expensive."

"What's your feeling about the contents?" Lionel carefully pulled the candlestick forward.

"Personally, I've never been enraptured with them. I appreciate their associations of course, and am surprised they are not a good deal more valuable than the museums people make out. But I don't share Drummond's romantic passion for it all." She paused again. "I'd have thought a responsible tenant could very well be the answer."

"There can be no solution which doesn't guarantee the contents remaining here, all the contents, and being protected. More than that, they'd need to be cherished." Sylvia placed both hands on the walnut surface in front of her. Made without emphasis, it was a trenchant gesture.

"How," inquired Gwen, addressing Lionel, "are you proposing we pay for these improvements? Even patching the roof here costs the earth."

"That's the crucial point." Lionel eased back. Remember now, he instructed himself, no bullying. No withering remarks. "The Royal Museum has, as you all realise, put us on the spot." He saluted the lofty ceiling. "Drummond and I made it clear that we were offering them the contents as a whole, so they could be kept together. They have come up with a different proposal. They want to acquire the Rossetti for display in Edinburgh. On that basis, and only on that basis, they would take over the archive and all the other moderately worthy objects with which the castle is loaded. They would look after them properly, which would be an enormous step forward. They would in effect be loaned back for display in situ, as they call it."

"How much can we realistically expect to get?" Gwen asked.

"For the Rossetti? They have hinted at about half a million. But of course they have Trustees to satisfy, and they want to take the picture to Edinburgh for examination. They suggest we agree on an independent adjudicator. Either that, or we appoint our own expert advisers, and they appoint theirs. A settlement would then be negotiated. Perhaps I should put my cards on the table at this point. I think we should retain Stewart Urquhart. He is immensely experienced. We could rely on him to look after our interests." Sylvia's hands were folded on the table. One of her thumbs began a gentle agitation against the other. Lionel added, "I also think Stewart would more than cover his fees by obliging the Museum to pay a realistic price for the Rossetti."

Iona laughed shortly. "I shall certainly not volunteer to take that picture down."

"Fogo," Gwen murmured, as the dog suddenly started to his feet and went to Sylvia and Lionel in turn, wagging for attention. "Come and sit down." Fogo nudged Iona in passing and returned grinning to Gwen's side. Then he made for one of the armchairs in which Sholto and Bryony had sat on either side of the fireplace. There he settled, curled up within a scrolling acanthus frame.

Sylvia said, "I can agree to lease Penwhapple to suitable people, supposing they exist. I must exercise the right to be consulted as to who qualifies." Her voice became more intense. "But on no account should our Rossetti go. The double portrait belongs here and nowhere else."

"I so sympathise with you, Sylvia." Gwen's fingers touched lightly on Sylvia's for a second. "None of us wants anything to change. But we must be realistic, as Iona says, for the sake of the younger generation. I'm sure that is Drummond's conviction."

"Has he ever discussed letting the Rossetti leave the castle?" Sylvia turned to face first Gwen, and then her brother.

It was Lionel who replied. "The last time we discussed the subject he stressed the importance of getting our strategy right. A Penwhapple that's vulnerable will be no good to Ricky and Tiffany. It's got to be properly managed for the next phase of its life. There is no sense, Sylvia, in keeping all these wonderful objects in an old tower house which hasn't any modern insulation, and only a half-baked alarm system."

"It's been perfectly satisfactory so far - apart, perhaps, for the central heating, which is a source of continual trouble. As for the portrait, you know that Sholto's death was caused by attempting to remove it. Surely if the Museum are prepared to leave everything else here they would be prepared to leave the double portrait."

"Perhaps we'd better drop that point for a moment." Lionel studied his nails. "Let me widen the discussion in a way we have so far avoided. There's the matter of the school's continued tenancy of Somersby House. Let us just ask ourselves how that might fit into the equation. Somersby has great potential, the kind of property that fetches between three and five hundred thousand in today's market." The expression his elder sister saw seemed to ask, did that hit the mark?

"I don't understand what you're talking about," she responded. "Are you suggesting we should break up a Trust which goes back well before our parents' day?"

"Selling would certainly give us wider scope," Iona said delicately.

Sylvia shot her a daunting look. She removed her hands from Gwen's reach and clenched them under the table. "Somersby is a way of life, a sacred trust. Ogier is a splendid teacher in Bryony's tradition. He is more than that. He is in a sense the true heir to Penwhapple."

There was silence, which Lionel found agreeable and the others disturbing.

Iona said, "We surely can't allow our feelings for Ogier to influence our decision. Everything is complicated enough already, heaven knows."

"That is not the point of what I was saying," retorted Sylvia.

Lionel adjusted his tone with a touch of unction. "It does not really help to be intransigent, Sylvia. Those of us with our own stakes in Penwhapple might decide to reconsider our interests. And incidentally, do we really need to talk about Ogier as if he was one of the family? He's a second cousin several times removed. I have no interest in his money, and fail to see why he should have an interest in mine."

Sylvia looked at him grimly. "No-one should suppose my own

stake in Penwhapple is cut and dried, or leaves out Ogier. You see, my concerns are quite different. If this place is let, will the school continue to have the use of the gardens, and the Rossetti pool? There must be no prejudice to Ogier's interests."

"Ogier is an excellent fellow, we all acknowledge that." Lionel glanced at Iona, on whom the elder sister's intervention had had its usual subduing effect. "We all experience poetic moments. Even I am not devoid of fine feelings. I began writing poems when everyone else did, I suppose - around three." He crossed his legs with energetic change of mood. "But we must be prosaic too. As far as the school is concerned, I shall be attending Trustee Meetings regularly in future, I assure you."

"I quite see the school should keep its access to Penwhapple's garden and other facilities," Iona managed to say. "Here we are, to take decisions on the family property. Perhaps we should stick to the status quo."

Lionel transferred his attention to her with the raised eyebrow usually reserved for Ricky. "What exactly are you saying, Iona?" He had a shrewd idea, and wanted to coax it into the open.

Iona prevaricated. "We four inherited the property, there's no going back on that, and long ago we made our own wishes clear. I see no advantage in going over it again with needless legal expense."

"You don't want Tiffany, or Ricky, to lose out in some sort of reshuffle," spelt out Lionel for his own purposes, and Iona's edification.

His sister uttered a mortified little laugh. "The less muddle there is, the better. Apart from which, Ricky and Tiffany are so fond of Penwhapple, so involved in it."

"Ogier is just as involved," said Sylvia staunchly. "Actively involved. But tell me, Lionel. What grounds have you for thinking a lease on Penwhapple would work? Have you other examples?"

"Yes," said Lionel quickly. "I can give you two or three very comparable examples where a house this size, or bigger, is rented out with total responsibility for upkeep. And where indeed the tenants have spent small fortunes over ten or twenty years on improving the property."

"What sort of people are we talking about? asked Gwen. "They sound enormously wealthy."

Lionel spread his hands. "People like Messrs Feinstein and

Lance. Americans or Canadians in at least one of the cases, a castle in Angus to be precise, which Americans revamped completely."

With her air of mild obstinacy Sylvia said, "I thought the whole point was to keep everything as it is." She felt dislocated between the creative past and a crude reality. The shock of her isolation had begun to neutralise her will. She walked to Sholto's chair and touched the carving on the top rail. Cave Canem, the family's assertive Border motto. With what seemed amusement, Fogo's eyes kindled from the opposite side of the fireplace. Sylvia sat down, distanced from her family, and stared at the dog. If only there could be some sign. Memories of her teaching days at Somersby invaded her heart. A great lethargy held her. Fogo's ears twitched.

Gwen's voice said with singsong insistence, "Drummond would be on Lionel's side, Sylvia dear! It isn't ideally what I'd like to have happen. But that's neither here nor there. I only want to support Drummond's wishes."

"You feel we should asset-strip more ruthlessly?" Lionel took her up with sharp tone and glance. "This may sound paternalistic, but a clean sweep might be in the younger generation's interests." He waited. Sylvia closed her eyes. "Or we could bring negotiations with the Royal Museum to a conclusion, one way or another. Which means smoking them out on the Rossetti. It would not tie us down, Sylvia. All I want is agreement to negotiate." He allowed himself a very small smile. No-one spoke. Lionel looked across at his sister. "What do you think, Sylvia? Do you at least accept that we should enter into further discussions?"

"And you say that would mean the portrait going to Edinburgh?"

"Yes, for technical evaluation. We would not be committed to a sale."

As if choosing death by a thousand cuts, Sylvia said, from Sholto's chair, "Very well, the portrait to go."

"And Stewart Urquhart? All agreed that we retain his services?" Again no-one spoke. Lionel waited. "From today's discussion I am more than ever convinced that we should have independent advice. Not put ourselves in the hands of those pachyderms at the Royal Museum." There was further silence. "That's agreed then. Now just one further point, and here, Sylvia, we are entirely in your hands. Could I authorise Ricky to show the Canadians round? Again, nothing irrevocable would be involved. They would be shown the castle as it has been shown to scores of other visitors. We would make that quite clear."

Sylvia somehow conveyed acquiescence.

"Well, that's very good of you. Ricky will show Messrs Feinstein and Lance over personally once a time has been agreed. Oh, yes, one other very minor point. Can Ricky go over the castle's security arrangements with you sometime? We're supposed to do this every year and haven't. The song and dance which the Royal Museum have made over security has been timely, in that sense at any rate."

Shortly after the visitors left Sylvia's telephone rang. She was still trying to come to terms with a new source of depression. In future Lionel would be attending Trustee Meetings. For a moment she thought the clipped voice on the line was his. It turned out to be something to do with the Procurator Fiscal. Proceedings against a certain Mr Hogarth, for transactions in cars.

"Well yes, he did drive a very nice old car himself, a Jaguar I think. He kept it in beautiful condition. He offered to sell it to me, but of course I wouldn't want a big car. Mr Hogarth is an excellent mechanic, and I am not."

"You knew him well then, Miss Moffat? I'm afraid it isn't just one old Jaguar. He is being accused of systematically dealing in cars and failing to pay tax on the transactions. Added to which the Procurator is leading evidence suggesting that Mr Hogarth showed little concern over the provenance of his vehicles. In other words, he is being accused of dealing in stolen goods."

"That's terrible. Mr Hogarth a" - Sylvia searched for the right word - "a fence? Really, I find that very hard to believe. He's always so polite and straightforward. He may have been foolish. But not dishonest."

"I'm sorry to say the Procurator has a contrasting view. I'll be doing my best on Mr Hogarth's behalf, of course, and my reason for telephoning is this. Would you be prepared to testify to his character? And would you appear in court if required?'

Sylvia's heart thumped unpleasantly. She began tentatively, "You see, Mr Hogarth's small boy has been coming here, and Mr Hogarth calls quite often I would say. Well, not often, it's too far to come, but fairly regularly." As she spoke Sylvia was remembering Iona's and Ogier's warnings about Hal. "I can vouch for the fact that he is concerned as a father." She paused, deep in thought "It's just that . . . " Again the lawyer waited. "Well, my feeling is that he does not always hold Antony in his consciousness."

"Does he not then?" came the lawyer's soft accents. "And would that be a serious failing?"

"I believe it might be better for you to speak to Ogier Boyd, at Somersby. As you probably know, Mr Hogarth used to work at the school until quite recently. Mrs Hogarth still teaches there. There are complications into which I have not felt it my place to enquire."

"He says he has known you for several years?"

"Oh yes, certainly, in the sense that I took an interest in him ever since he and Mrs Hogarth first joined the school."

"I see. Quite a good time then." The lawyer reflected. "As a matter of fact, Miss Moffat, I have spoken to Mr Boyd. He is unwilling to come forward."

"Did he say why?"

"He appreciated my point that he might be too literal, as it were, about my client."

"Then I shall speak for Mr Hogarth, poor man. I shall want to consult Mr Boyd first, and hear his views. But I shall not change my mind."

"That's most kind of you. My client will be very grateful. I will come back to you if there are developments. Perhaps that will be best."

Sylvia dosed herself with arnica and made some herb tea. She passed a few moments looking into the swaying mass of oak and Scots pine in the gorge. Hooded crows were slanging each other from their midst. Above the gorge the house martins were massing, restless for the autumn migration. Sylvia thought of Christina Rossetti, coming to Penwhapple for the first time, innocent of its spell and its burdens. Carrying her tea to the bedroom, she dialled Ogier.

"I hear that Hal Hogarth is in trouble with the police. What I don't understand is why you won't put in a good word for the wretched fellow."

"I have in fact already been interviewed by the police, and I can assure you that I spoke very positively about Hal. I miss his contribution to Somersby. But, Sylvia, the College as a whole think it would do the school no good to get involved. You know how quick the media are with damaging innuendo. This is being too sensitive, in my personal view, but I do feel anxious. I wouldn't say this to the other Trustees, and usually at Michaelmas one is filled with confidence. For various reasons I feel less optimistic this year."

"But what are your honest feelings about Hal Hogarth? Is he a fence, as that nice lawyer put it? Could he have been stealing cars and selling them? I wish now I hadn't said he was such a good mechanic."

"We all know how volatile Hal is. He could just possibly have become involved in something shady. The temptation may have been there and he may have been drawn in. I doubt it, but it's possible."

"It doesn't change my position, Ogier. If I'm asked I'll speak up for him."

"We will both speak for him if we are called." Ogier kept silent for a moment. "You know, much as I admire your courage and loyalty, Sylvia, I wouldn't be happy to let you volunteer yourself for an appearance in Court. It would be most unwise. Your age and your medical condition would be some protection but not much, I fear."

"I'd survive! I'm looking forward to it already. There now. I think you are quite right to feel protective about the school."

"Actually, it's something more mundane that's worrying me, something I hesitate to mention. You may think this premature, but we are going to need another family Trustee. For various reasons neither Ricky or Gwen will do. It's a great pity Tiffany has moved to London. But it's only a matter of four meetings a year, and perhaps she could manage. I would like to get her on now, so she's there for the budget meeting in January. If the proposal had your backing, Sylvia, I'm sure it would go through."

"Yes," said Sylvia vaguely, "I too have been worrying about the Trustees. I won't let Lionel become Chairman, you know. I'd rather take that again myself if necessary. You see, there's the link with Penwhapple to consider. I regard your place as very important, Ogier. And as far as Tiffany is concerned, I am fully prepared to consider that option."

He said reassuringly, "We have to move with the times. Penwhapple is important to the school of course. But don't let that dictate your feelings. Take a decision on its merits."

"Now, that's a very good point." Sylvia paused. "What about you, Ogier? I could say a similar thing to you."

"You could?"

"The young teacher, Pippa Cursiter. I expect she's becoming a force to be reckoned with. She's got presence. But what lies behind it?"

"I think she's a very positive influence. Contributes forcefully at College meetings, which tends to antagonise Samantha. But Pippa's convictions are nothing if not sincere. She remembers something you said to her on that score."

"I have great respect for Samantha. Next to you, she is the one who most truly carries Somersby." It seemed an ideal chance to voice what had been a private impulse for some while. "Don't be bamboozled, Ogier. Pippa Cursiter seems so very strong-willed, and aware of making a powerful effect. But she hasn't Samantha's integrity. She may seek to make her mark and then move off. Not be Somersby material at all."

"You speak seriously."

"I do. But with all my life in motion, this is only a trifle after all."

"Don't worry." Ogier sounded uneasy." I value Samantha's integrity as much as you do, though it can become rather wearing." He cleared his throat. "As for Hal Hogarth, I've decided to spoil your fun. I'll telephone his lawyer and promise to give a warm personal reference, never mind the College."

Sylvia brought the conversation to a close. She sat with her cold cup of tea, thinking of the double portrait. She thought of Antony, starting in the Lower School. His visits to Penwhapple would have to be less frequent. Perhaps they could develop a new routine. Change was certainly in the air, if Tiffany was to be considered for the Trustees. Sylvia did wonder if she wasn't too inexperienced and young.

She felt sorry for Iona. Iona would miss Tiffany, now she was in London.

Chapter 11

With Antony full of excitement and in close attendance, Sylvia led Ricky to the rear of the tower. She pointed to the lancet which lit the undercroft, part of Sholto Moffat's remodelling. "So you're telling me we should have bars put there?"

"My dear old Aunt, yes, I'm convinced you should. Not only there but in all the ground floor windows. Someone small enough could easily squeeze through this one."

"Yes, if they had some objection to walking in at the front door." Sylvia was exasperated. "For years I have never locked the front door. Now I'm told to put bars on windows that have never been unlocked. Bryony's Joyous Guard is to become a prison."

Ricky laid a hand on his aunt's shoulder. "You must get bars fixed, just for your peace of mind. If you didn't, and anyone got in, there could conceivably be, well, difficulties with the insurance. I put it no higher than that." He gave the brat Antony a conniving look.

"Could you squeeze through yourself?" Sylvia demanded. "Wait here. I'll go round and open up."

"You can do it, can't you?" said Antony.

"I've no intention of trying," was Ricky's reply.

Presently Sylvia pushed the window open and called, "Just see if you can break in. I'll wager you can't."

Ricky made a pretence of hitching himself off the ground.

"That's no good," Sylvia urged. "You're a burglar! You've set your heart on stealing my belongings."

"I got my head through. That suggests the castle could be penetrated at this point. Dear old aunt, I am sporting my father's best silk tie and a pair of new shoes. I have an important meeting for which I need to look my best."

"You'd certainly make a feeble thief."

"Very well, I do not wish to say this, but think of infant crime.

Here, you, Childe or whatever you call yourself. Up you go." Ricky grabbed the squirming Antony and lifted him to the window. In an instant the delighted boy was through. Another instant and he was squirming back, covered in dirt. From the front of the castle came the sound of a vehicle and other activity. Antony rushed off to investigate.

Sylvia reappeared. "But why bars? We went to all that expense putting security locks on the windows. When will these insurance people be satisfied?"

"Do not blame me, Beldame of Ancient Wisdom. Blame the Royal Museum. Their views on security are incredible. Look, I will report back to Dad. If the smallest of the ground floor windows is vulnerable, presumably the rest are. I had better get off to this interesting appointment of mine. Cool, calm and collected. I will borrow a clothes brush, as there isn't time for a bath."

"You have an appointment? On a Sunday?"

"On a Sunday."

"What is this mysterious appointment?"

"Ah, I'm glad to have roused your curiosity. Something rather shameful."

"Dear me, where is Antony?

Speculation was forestalled by Antony's reappearance. "Auntie Sylvia! Aunt Sylvia, come quickly. Come and see the trees!"

Feeling stoical, they trudged up to the forecourt.

An old horse lorry was parked on the apron. Around it stood a quantity of pot-grown trees and shrubs. "All yours," said Hal Hogarth. He stepped backwards, gesturing like a conjurer. "They've got their name tags on," he added. From his cheerful demeanour no-one could have guessed he had criminal proceedings hanging over him.

"Mr Hogarth, I'm crippled with arthritis! Do you imagine I can dig that lot into my garden?"

"Of course not. You'll get help. Some nice specimens there. Specialist nursery selling up."

"You wouldn't help me, I suppose."

"No. But they'll go in, and you'll be well pleased with your instant garden." He went to the cab, wiping earth off his hands. "I sold the Jag last week. Someone got a bargain there. Maybe I should have dumped your plants on the lawn. Never mind, it's done now."

"Look, Aunt Sylvia, I will really have to dash." Ricky glanced with distaste at the plants. "Assuming I can reverse through this jungle. You won't forget I'm bringing Miss Lance and Miss Feinstein on Tuesday, will you? Day after tomorrow. No guided tour, Dad insists. I've mugged it all up and can manage, no problem. It would be nicer if the place didn't look like a market garden when we drove up. First impressions can be rather important."

Ricky departed, the secret of his afternoon appointment still intact. He had offered to let Pippa drive the BMW, and had been taken seriously. Rather a humourless girl. As Ricky reversed expertly round the horse lorry he felt agreeably caddish. He would have enjoyed telling Sylvia that junior staff at Somersby were into performance cars.

Sylvia turned to Hal. "Come in and have a coffee. You can talk to Antony while we drink it."

Hal pulled an antique hunter from his dungarees. He was wearing coloured socks and handsome country shoes. On his head he wore a knitted circular cap. Thick curly hair radiated from it like a screen of roses. They passed the mural. "Needs a spot of touching up," he commented. "Can't you get a conservation grant?"

"It's not that simple, alas." Sylvia paused in front of the opening scene of the King's Quair. Soldiers walked beneath the emprisoned King's window. One of them was an informal portrait of Arthur Hughes, another of Holman-Hunt. In the foreground the walls of Windsor Castle were suggested, complete with mediaeval grotesques. In the background, an assortment of towers and turrets and battlements. A minion could be seen extinguishing the night flare on a distant watch tower. Sholto was said to have modelled this figure on himself. "He used to dissolve wax in turpentine,"Sylvia commented. "You can see. It has a sort of glow. But damp is the enemy. Sheets of zinc were needed to line the walls." Forgetting about coffee, Sylvia moved up the stairs. Antony drifted away. "There you have poor James the First glimpsing Lady Jane Beaufort in the garden. Christina Rossetti was the model for Lady Jane. There is just a little doubt about that. Her brother William is the second of the three courtiers, quite unmistakable. The others are Swinburne, unmistakable too, and Sholto himself. That's Sholto again in the saucy green hat, feeding Bryony's real life pet duck. He put himself in several of the menial roles."

Hal chuckled and shook his head. He consulted his hunter again. "Hey, look at the time. I'd better pay my respects to Annie pretty quick. I'm to be in Kilmarnock for lunch."

"What do I owe you?"

"Owe me?"

"For the shrubs."

"Not a lot." They went into the kitchen. Hal fumbled in a pocket, as though looking for the bill. "Tell you what, you pay for the petrol and we'll call it quits. Twenty-five pounds, not bad, eh? I could probably pick up a couple of stone urns cheap if you like. Some nice little cherubs too, and a pair of dolphins?"

"I haven't got twenty-five pounds at present. Not handy. But I'll let you have it next time." Sylvia lifted the lid of a cheese dish. "Wait a minute, here's five, no, six. I'd rather square up now."

"That's a respectable dish. Very nice." Hal raised an eyebrow at its contents. "Good morning, Annie." He gave her his attractive smile. Annie turned to the sink.

"You haven't seen what Mr Hogarth has produced," Sylvia said. "I'm going to SOS Pat. We'll need half Somersby to plant us out."

"Where's Ant then?" Hal asked.

"He's like the shifting wind, that one," Annie responded. She began making coffee, clattering the saucepan.

"I'll nip up," Hal said. He disappeared.

"And you'd best be nipping after him," was Annie's baleful advice. "It's a right scunner, having him about."

"We'll have coffee in here, Annie." Sylvia thought, yes, she would go up. Not to shadow Hal, just to see what Antony was doing. "I do wish you would not use that word, Annie." Annie busied herself at the cooker. "I say that because it is important to use words correctly. We, of all people, owe this to our native tongue."

Guided by the sound of their voices, Sylvia eventually found Hal and Antony outside the summer parlour. The climb had made her out of breath. Hal was gazing pensively at Sholto's decoration of the rafters. Serpents and fish, birds, garlanded leaves. "That dining room of yours. Have you ever considered selling the table and chairs?"

"Never," said Sylvia. "That furniture is inseparable from my family and the house."

"And the picture?"

"The double portrait? Certainly not!" Sylvia led the way back into the room with its painting of Bryony and Sholto, the heroic flag behind them, the dog at their feet. The magical glimpse of Ailsa Craig. Above the portrait, in Sholto's lettering, the famous inscription:

Move. Not. This. Picture. Let. It. Be.
For. Love. Of. Those. In. Effigy.

"Nice picture," Hal ran a finger down the frame. "Wouldn't have chosen a gilt frame myself." They retraced their steps to the Turkey-carpeted landing. "You don't believe there's really a curse on selling it, do you?" He halted. "I thought there were some shrews on the ceiling somewhere."

"There are three moles on the cornice in the laird's bedroom," replied Sylvia, absently. She was thinking, of course there was a curse on selling the painting, and even on moving it.

"The laird's bedroom. That'll be it then." Hal nodded sagely. He remembered the moles now. White stomachs, out of scale, snouts pointed skywards. "What about the laird's bed?" One of the endposts of the Penwhapple bed was crowned with a monkey playing the bagpipes, the other with a bear. Hal reckoned he could raise three thousand on the bed alone. The pair of sixteenth century Moffat tocher chairs would fetch another fifteen hundred. Good rustic carving there.

"What about it?" demanded Sylvia.

"You don't fancy a more hygienic type of bed? I could get you two thou for your fancy one."

"The very idea!" Sylvia exclaimed. When had Hal Hogarth been into her bedroom? "We had better go after Antony," she said.

"Do you have any furniture that's not part of the fittings?" Hal asked, before it was too late.

"For sale? Nothing." They found Antony in the kitchen with Annie. "Have you time for coffee?" Sylvia asked, remembering Kilmarnock.

The watch with its handsome silver case made a third appearance. Hal indicated the cheese dish. "Any more where that came from?"

He tapped his breast pocket, cocking his head hopefully.

Sylvia frowned. "Didn't I pay you?" She faltered. "No, you're quite right. I still owe you nineteen pounds." She lifted another pottery lid. "I'll have to go upstairs. I won't be long."

"Don't hurry." Hal addressed himself to Annie's unsociable back. "Come on, Annie. Tell us about the Curse of Penwhapple."

Hal left soon after Sylvia produced the remaining money. Not a word was said about prison, or bail, or Sylvia's readiness to speak up for him in court. Yet she felt he had tried to tell her about these things and, to some extent, succeeded. A date for the trial had not been fixed. There was some suggestion that the charges might be withdrawn. Sylvia felt tranquil. Sometime after lunch she decided to walk Antony home. Returning from Somersby, she met Pippa on the drive. They exchanged a few pleasantries.

Pippa said, "Miss Moffat, I've never forgotten the talk we had when I arrived at Somersby last year. What you told me then has always seemed to lie at the very heart of child-centred education. It's meant even more to me as I have come to understand Somersby better."

She prolonged the conversation for a while, Sylvia saying little. Her mind was full of the contrariness of life. The pity of a child, whose parents could not share him together.

Iona had prepared bobotie for dinner, which they ate early. The sisters joked about this dish, supposing it "impossible to spoil." It had become a favourite of Antony's. "Knowing you, I'm surprised he isn't here to share it with us," said Iona. "How is the new arrangement working?"

"Very well. I do homework with him three times a week, and it can be helpful if I have him when Alison's on weekend duty. But it's early days yet. By the way, did I mention that Ogier wanted to make Tiffany a Trustee? Doesn't that strike you as surprising?"

Iona went over to the tiny window seat. There was a perceptible pause. "I think Tiffany would make a very good Trustee. She loves coming back so much. Last year it was as if she had never left."

"Precisely. She needs a break from the school. When she knows who she really is she can come back to it again. I thought it was unfair of Ogier, unlike him. Unfair to Tiffany, I mean."

"Surely, Tiffany might be allowed to decide that for herself."

"She's too young. Don't smile in that superior way. I'll tell you what I have done. You know I was planning to leave everything I have to Tiffany and Ricky equally. I'm fond of Ricky, he's such fun, but I've decided to adjust that slightly. I'm going to make Tiffany sole beneficiary of my reversionary interest in Somersby."

Iona heard this with mixed feelings. She began working out how to persuade Sylvia to leave Tiffany something more tangible.

Sylvia said, "Walk back to the castle with me. There's a change I want to show you before it gets dark."

They made their way slowly up the drive, coming on Hal Hogarth's trees only as they turned the final bend. When Iona reacted with predictable dismay, Sylvia seemed reassured. "Actually, I don't mind," she told her sister. "Nothing bothers me these days. Trust you to take a dim view."

"You'll bother when you're wracked with sciatica all winter."

"Nonsense. I don't intend to do any of the work. Ogier will let me have a contingent. He'll come himself if I know him."

"Well, count me out. I think that man Hogarth has a colossal cheek. I'd have told him to take them all away! What did he charge for them?"

"Twenty-five pounds."

"Twenty-five pounds! It's obvious they're stolen. You can't fill the grounds with stolen property. Where on earth are you going to put them? They'll alter the whole character of the garden."

"I thought they might be stolen too, to begin with. But Mr Hogarth convinced me they're not. They're his way of saying thank you. I hope they ask me to appear in Court, don't you? I don't believe for a minute Mr Hogarth would do a scam, as they call it. He's not the type."

For a moment Iona was acutely aware of why Lionel had always accused his sisters of being large and literal. "I wish you'd stay the night at the Lodge with me," she said. "You're right, I do miss Tiffany." Carefully, Iona changed direction. "I should like to talk about your idea of leaving her some of your money. I regret having Tiffany so late in life. Now I feel old enough to be her grandmother!"

"Oh, maybe you do now, but it was different earlier. We're both apt to be melancholic these days. Perhaps we should take cannabis. I'm sure Hal Hogarth does."

"Do tell the Court that," Iona expostulated. "Appearing as a witness with your heart condition, it's outrageous, Sylvia, and you know it. I want to learn exactly how Mr Hogarth got hold of all these trees." She looked around the forecourt. "Bother the man! And with the Canadians coming on Tuesday, too!"

Chapter 12

Ricky swept past the entrance to Somersby on his way to meet the ladies known in Moffat and Moffats as Messrs Lance and Feinstein. Noisily decelerating, he startled Iona as she planted bulbs in her garden.

His meeting with Pippa on Sunday had got off to an unpromising start. Having settled herself behind the wheel of his car as if she owned it, she had taken the New Daily intersection at speed and without regard for traffic precedence. Ricky thought she was going to roll them down the grassy embankment. Then, on the back roads to Drongan, she had demonstrated the distinction between 'cornering' and merely going round corners. Once on the main road she sailed past the parade of Sunday drivers while they hooted at her. It was with a sense of relief rather than anticipation that Ricky gave her directions to a small restaurant overlooking the Heads of Ayr.

It was not possible to get one of the tables with the famous view. They found themselves overlooking an intimately enclosed courtyard instead. On a plinth extolling the virtues of the Ayrshire cow stood a concrete example of the breed, realistically painted. It was near enough to make out the words someone had written on the udder in black felt-tip: Mechanised Power, No Thanks.

Ricky raised an eyebrow, in the manner perfected by his father. "The human touch?" An image of the Corstorphine chiropodist bent over his grisly work invaded his mind. "Tell me, what sort of a father was yours? When you were growing up?" Pippa was regarding him steadily. "Was he the hands on sort?" The waiter took their order. Ricky renewed his efforts. "I mean, did your father interfere with you much?" No, that was not what he meant either. Pippa, uttering a half laugh, turned back to the cow. A robin had perched on its rump. Ricky dashed his hair aside, saying, "I've missed my vocation."

"As a diplomat?" She remained in profile, adding distantly, "Never mind. You can always be a driving instructor." Suddenly facing him, she smiled. "What a super drive that was, Ricky. It's a while since I felt so stimulated."

This was more encouraging. Ricky resumed his questions, probing to discover what sort of teenager she had been. She answered in her serious manner, carefully considering what she said and pleased to be drawn out. If she was a touch complacent, Ricky didn't mind. Her gentle attempts at accuracy amused him. They had ordered coffee when a bright young voice behind them said, "Ricky! Hello! How are you doing then?" - and it was Amy Wilson, with whom Ricky had pursued an on-off liaison for years. Pippa saw a tall, well-groomed girl in expensive trousers and a sweater. As Ricky tried to stand Amy embraced him lavishly and forced him back on his chair. "Don't let me interrupt. I've just been perching on a bar stool next door and I thought, Wicked, there's Ricks." Her glance passed to Pippa and back to Ricky. He hastily introduced them. Amy indicated the open doorway. "My dear Mama is repairing her face. I'm actually on my way to see Hamish. You remember Hamish? Just back from Canton, lucky beast."

Ricky did remember Hamish. Well muscled, well heeled.

"Must trot," Amy said. Wiggling a finger at Pippa and rumpling Ricky's head, she sauntered towards the hall.

"She's attractive. An old flame?"

"Not likely." Ricky swung round on his chair, seeking the waitress. He could feel Pippa presuming his eyes were following Amy. "Could you bring our coffees, please? Time is running a bit short." He grinned at Pippa. "A giddy chick if ever there was one. And Dear Mama is fairly terrifying." He tried to resume his urbane question and answer game but found Pippa less sporting. As he fished for suitable coins to leave on the tablecloth she told him he would have done well in the Spanish Inquisition. She gave him another of her spontaneous smiles.

Ricky turned into the forecourt of Penwhapple to meet his Canadians, and was confronted by the muddy reality of Hal's trees. Josephine and Gloria had already arrived. Gloria was rearranging herself after getting out of their tourer. She carried a spectacular bunch of flowers, gift-wrapped with trailing ribbons. Josephine, stringing Gloria's camera around her own neck, strolled over to have a look at the ravine. She lifted a hand. "Does anyone go walking in that wilderness?" she called.

"Good afternoon, Miss Feinstein, you seem to have arrived a little early. Yes, my Aunt walks there every day, wearing lethal rubber boots. If you've time we'll go there too."

"It's your time, my friend," Josephine said warmly, landing a capable hand on his arm. "We've all the time in the world, haven't we Glo? Not that time exists up here."

"Well, shall we look at the garden? There is quite a lot of it. The part around the house is what we call the aesthetic movement garden. Rather fine," Ricky assured her, "were it not for the chaos. We like to keep everything up. The walled garden has a more formal, Victorian character. The ravine you were looking at extends to some nine acres. More of a romantic place. You'll like it. As a matter of fact I was down there myself this summer. There's a pool you can swim in."

"Maybe we should see the castle before taking on the garden."

"Excellent. Well, I'm sure my aunt will be ready for us." They made for the studded door. It opened suddenly, before Ricky could pull on the bell. It was Annie. With some formality, Ricky asked her if Sylvia was ready for them.

"She isn't far away."

"She is expecting us, I take it? It's all right if I show the visitors round?" Ricky found himself having to explain who the visitors were.

"You're expected, right enough. Miss Moffat's in the library, giving the scholar his homework. You're to leave that room till last."

"Oh, that's fine. Thanks, Annie."

Annie departed unwillingly. Gloria fingered the glazed lattice door to the main stair. Ricky indicated the stairway down. "The old undercroft, part of the original tower house. Later converted into a wine cellar but not used as such by my aunt. Easily reinstated."

"Surely," said Josephine, nodding briskly. They descended, and spent more time than Ricky had expected looking around. When they returned to the entrance hall it became necessary to adjust Ricky's original plan. Instead of proceeding to the library he took the stairs to the laird's bedroom in the secondary tower. The endposts of the Penwhapple bed suggested mild debauchery.

Josephine poked her head into the bathroom. The tub was stained with ancient water marks. "This too could be transformed without difficulty. You might like us to install a jacuzzi for you," Ricky said.

Behind him Gloria was examining the wallpaper. She commented on "the drapes" and asked who had composed the inscription for the trellised ceiling. Ricky decided to treat this as a rhetorical question. He escorted them to the banqueting hall. "The eighteen eighty-three addition," he announced, embarking on a short, intrepid lecture. Josephine and Gloria poked about separately, glancing at some pictures, studying those they favoured. Now and then each called for the attention of the other, ignoring Ricky's presence. "That's a coffered ceiling," Ricky advised them with an off-hand glance at his notes.

"Is there anything as prosaic as a kitchen?" Gloria inquired. "There must be some snag to all this splendour."

"Yes, right here, adapted by my aunt from the butler's pantry. Now, before we go in, I must warn you. What you are going to see is rather basic. But if you took a lease we would be delighted to do it up. Ah, Annie, how very encouraging to see tea things laid out."

Annie sat at the deal table. She sensed an atmosphere of judgment. These were not the usual visitors who came to admire Penwhapple and go away again.

"It's not exactly hi-tech," Ricky observed quietly. "But as I say, there would be no difficulty over remodelling."

"I should say not," conceded Gloria, absently. They moved on. Annie gave him a small smile. On the main staircase they paused. "Now this is the mural which my father mentioned. It illustrates a poem written by James the First called The King's Quair and is very well-known in artistic circles. My aunt could tell you more about it but if you want an amateur appreciation I'll be delighted to try." Josephine stood captivated, silently fingering the straps of Gloria's camera. Ricky recalled her joyous cry of luscious damsels and cute pageboys. He said, not wholly insincerely, "That's a section I've always liked. All those turrets and towers."

"And the figures," said Gloria. "They're so individual. You can tell he painted them from life."

"This," Ricky pointed, "is certainly the artist himself, in the guise of a gardener. I can identify the duck too. It was a pet of my great aunt's called Quasi." Slowly they continued upwards. Ricky felt he was acquitting himself well. At the head of the grand stair he ushered them into the summer parlour, encouraging them not to miss the view towards Ailsa Craig. If they wanted to exclaim over the landscape they could could do so now.

"Oh!" Gloria breathed. "Is it ever beautiful!"

"Is it ever," echoed her devoted companion.

"Another oak coffered ceiling," Ricky continued. "And that's our famous Rossetti." He awaited the cries of ecstatic veneration which this painting usually provoked.

"I like the dog," Gloria said. "Freaky little fellow."

"Mr Moffat," Josephine asked in sterner tones. "Are these really the original chairs and table?"

"Everything's original,' An expression of disbelief crossed Miss Feinstein's face. Ricky began to adjust his perception of the visitors. With mounting misgivings he took them to join Sylvia in the library. Antony was sulking in the corner. No good sending him to hurry the tea. Ricky went himself, uneasily aware that his aunt was addressing the visitors in her sing song voice. Bad sign.

"The oak cabinet was constructed by my cousin, Sholto Moffat," she was saying. "Well, I call him my cousin but of course he was really a great-uncle. He never married. He used mainly late mediaeval and early renaissance oak panels, and they conceal the fifteenth century entrance to the tower. At that time it was on first floor level, of course, as was the common practice in Border strongholds."

Ricky did not delay in the kitchen. When he and Annie got back to the library with the tea things, Gloria was talking. "This seems the perfect gentrification of something genuinely antique. We want a spot of privacy, Miss Moffat. Some space. Shall I tell you what it's like here? It's just like fairyland."

"How very perceptive. Our cousin Sholto compared Penwhapple with the palace of the Sleeping Beauty, in its enchanted and limitless repose. Which I dare say it then enjoyed."

"It's cozy for a castle," said Josephine. "But do you freeze in winter?"

"Certainly not!" said Sylvia stoutly. She occupied herself briskly with pouring the tea.

Antony had got over his sulk. "I'll take you up on the tower," he suggested, emerging from the corner turret.

"You can offer the biscuits to everyone," Sylvia told him.

"I don't think we'll have time for the tower." Josephine glanced at her watch, then at Gloria. "Another day?"

Sylvia gave Ricky a stricken glance. She turned to Gloria, apparently the more sympathetic of her visitors. "I'm sorry I haven't been able to help in your search for a home. Perhaps this place will have given you some ideas."

"It's given us so many ideas we'll never realise them any place else."

"I hope I won't seem rude not coming down. I look forward to your Scottish cook book."

Gloria adopted an ingratiating expression. "Could I beg a favour? Might I take one interior photograph? Just something that will bring all this back?" She glanced rapidly round. "How about one of you, Miss Moffat, in front of the family portrait? That was such a nice, light room."

Sylvia did not want to appear disobliging on the point of getting rid of her visitors. "I don't see why not," she responded. Labouring a little over the stairs, she led the way to the summer parlour. Josephine hovered by the door while her friend organised the shot. "Get her to move a shade more to the right, Glo," she suggested.

Moving as requested, Sylvia exposed the entire double portrait. The camera clicked, then clicked again. Ricky began to feel uneasy. He should have ruled out photographs, especially featuring the Rossetti. He felt a hand being shyly inserted into his. It was the brat. Ricky declined to look down. He gave Antony's hand a squeeze, then spoke emphatically. There should be no more photographs inside the house. Sylvia retreated to the window, relieved to give no further concessions. Ricky escorted his visitors downstairs, Antony following in a series of dangerous jumps. When they emerged on the forecourt the little boy ran out, looking up at the tower and pointing. "There's a little dog lives up there," he informed them.

Gloria now confronted Ricky as she had confronted his Aunt. "Can we trespass on your good nature another short while?" She waved the camera. "Could we have a glimpse of the garden? What say, Jo?" Her eyes darted from side to side.

"Very well then," Ricky responded, with a sharpness that he instantly modified. "We'll start with the aesthetic movement garden."

"What must it be like in the evening?" Josephine enthused. "So lovely it would hurt." She led them forward, ducking round a group of ancient apple trees. "Why don't you take the greenhouse?" she suggested. "Just look at the stork up there, Gloria." As though posed expressly for their purpose, a lead stork perched in an angle of the enclosing wall. From it a metal bower made an arch over the path.

"There's another one," Antony informed them. "They're twins."

The storks duly photographed, Gloria began measuring distances with her eye and making still greater discoveries. "Know what I'm thinking, Jo? I can't wait to have a shot of you with the castle in the background. It's got such atmosphere, it's unbelievable."

"Show Mr Moffat how to use the camera. He can get us both in."

"Great idea. Give me the camera a minute, Glo." Josephine squinted into it while giving directions. "Far out! Now, I want to catch the shadows just where they are. Left arm bent, Glo, stand forward with your left foot planted firmly, knee a bit bent, OK? Look out into the trees to the left. Now, Mr Moffat! Everything's set. I'll get in the picture, all you have to do is press this button." She handed Ricky the camera and went across to stand Miss Lance in the angle of her arm. They gazed into the distance together.

More pictures followed. Eventually they found themselves back at the bright white tourer. Gloria said, "It's tempting providence, Josephine. You steal some pictures from the garden, and you never get to see the place again. That's how it goes."

With some formality Ricky helped them into the car and presided over Miss Feinstein's manoeuvring in the forecourt.

"Come here, Childe of the Pits," he ordered, as the car turned out of sight. He grasped Antony by a wrist and an ankle. He swung him round, fast, and dumped him on the damp grass.

"More, more!"

"More, detestable brat? I'll give you more, then!"

"Ricky! Stop it at once, you'll make him sick. Come now, Childe, back to Somersby." It was Sylvia. She carried Antony's coat and a satchel in which he kept his homework. Very little homework had been done that afternoon.

"Old Trout, it's been a long day for you. As an earnest of Moffat and Moffats' goodwill I will return him to Somersby for you. How would you like that, brat? I'll let you steer my BMW."

Sylvia fell in with this proposal with relief, Antony with delight. The Moffat private agenda was to see Pippa again. This did not work out. Pippa was busy in the staff room. Ricky did not see her. But she saw him, returning a happy little boy to his mother. She was always to remember that brief glimpse of Ricky, elegant, trustworthy, good with children. Years later, the memory still had power to charm and hurt her.

As he drove back to Ayr, Ricky took stock. His good old aunt had disliked the visitors. He thought they were all right, with their photography and their cookbooks and their designer label clothes. Hard nosed, of course, but that could be an advantage. Having them as tenants was the snag. He had known it wouldn't work. They were not going to become unofficial curators of a Pre-Raphaelite past. They wanted to put their own mark on Penwhapple. Sylvia wouldn't even consider them. And now he had to report to his father.

Photography. That was the angle. Sketch the afternoon's proceedings amusingly, but let fall that the visitors had photographed the Rossetti. Wind his father up a bit. Stiffen his resolve to sell. Ridiculous hanging on to the Rossetti, with all that money involved.

With his share Ricky planned to get a GTi like Miss Feinstein's.

Chapter 13

"Sure you'll be all right?' Lionel repeated. He placed a solicitous hand on Sylvia's shoulder. They had met, by arrangement, at Iona's Lodge. He wanted her out of the way while the Rossetti was collected from the castle.

"Perfectly all right, Lionel. Given that today will be the nadir of my life."

Almost two months had passed since Hal Hogarth had delivered his trees and shrubs. They were still where he had left them, but rearranged into more orderly groups. The shrubs were a disappointment, lilac and buddleia mostly. The trees included some unusual specimens, a katsura and a mulberry, which would need sheltering, and four slow-growing, paper-bark maples. Criminal charges against Hal had been dropped, so Sylvia was not to play the starring role in a courtroom melodrama after all. She now had the uncomfortable impression that perhaps Hal was a thief.

Lionel lifted the hand with which he had rallied Sylvia. "Let Iona look after you. And forgive me for saying this yet again, but she is quite right about those trees. They're an eyesore. It's time they went." He let himself out of the front door. Cozy little place, the Lodge. Must be worth, at a conservative guess, what? Two bedrooms and only one bathroom. Small garden. Perhaps not that much after all. About thirty-five thousand? At least Sylvia would be out of the way there for an hour or two.

Lionel strode along the drive, enjoying the earthy smells intensified by recent rain. There were puddles in the potholes. He stood in the forecourt and surveyed the castle. The bell house stood bleakly against a bank of low cloud. If his Victorian forebears were paying due attention, that self-important bell would peal a solemn protest today. Lionel wandered towards the glen and stared into its wet foliage, hands in pockets. He glanced at his watch, returned to the castle and walked inside, running lightly up the short flight of entrance stairs. Penwhapple had charm, he admitted to himself. The panelled landings off the stair turret, for example, panels worth a good deal on their own. The shallow carpeted stair, very decent and snug. The decorated architraves he liked less, for all their birds and beasts and flowers. He paused before the bust of Sholto. It gazed across him and through the deep window. Lionel felt ignored. In an act of solidarity, he looked with Sholto through the slanted opening.

Scottish baronial, Lionel decided, had never been to his taste. He had an aversion to turrets, caphouses, corbels, oriels and bartizans. An Edwardian villa would be more his line. They had learnt how to make themselves comfortable by then. He watched the corbies flapping from the oak trees. He thought he heard a car approach. Whistling nervously, Lionel climbed further up and paused at another window. He wished someone would come. Five minutes later a car nosed into view and reversed in the forecourt. Lionel descended in a leisurely manner to conduct its driver inside.

"Hello! Mr Moffat?" The hand which Lionel clasped was tiny. "Jane Hardie. From the Museum."

"Goodness, I expected a brawny male! I'm Lionel Moffat, Miss Moffat's brother."

Preceding him up the stairs, Miss Hardie chattered away with engaging friendliness. "Surely people don't expect brawny males any more. Not politically correct." She was the slightest thing Lionel had ever seen, not much above five feet, exuding energy and confidence, an Assistant Keeper, whatever that meant. He trailed her to the summer parlour, fielding her comments on the mural, fascinated by her quick, light feet in their heavy shoes. Under one arm she seemed to be carrying a shroud.

"Right, if you go in there," he guided, leaning past to open the door. "This is the room. And there is the double portrait."

The young woman went boldly to examine it. "Most eccentric." She smiled over to Lionel, to show there were no hard feelings. "I mean, typically so. It evokes that ambitious picture, La Pia de' Tolomei. He's got the same verdant countryside in the background, but very low key. And such character in the figures. Her folded hands on his shoulder are charming." She peered closer. "The tower wall is unexpected. Again, very like La Pia. He wasn't considered much good at walls." She studied the details in silence, with Lionel just behind her. "There's a lot of emotion. Not Rossetti's usual dreamy stuff, either, more sense of purpose. I quite see why you're expecting so much for it. A wonderful pendant to our other Rossetti."

"They were intelligent and cultivated people I suppose." Lionel pointed to the brass-bound telescope in Sholto's hand. "I've always enjoyed that detail. As you say, there's a sense of purpose about them."

"I like his natty pink suit and stripy stockings." Miss Hardie smiled. "And his expression is lovely. As for the lady, she's evidently inspired, looking out to sea. That's Ailsa Craig?"

"Or the Fortunate Isle, as our friends called it."

The girl cocked her head to one side. "Her garments are intriguing. Very serious, with the chaste white collar and those billowing sleeves."

"I shall miss the flag when the picture's gone. It always puts me in a healthy frame of mind. The dog too."

"Yes, he's lovely. He manages to convey something very forthright about them all."

Lionel drew a screwdriver from his pocket. "Well, the moment has come!" He proffered the handle with a flourish, wagging it up and down. "I'm sure you have a way with pictures. One somehow assumes they're as temperamental as their creators."

His companion appeared humorously nonplussed. "I don't know how deft I am with those things." She dropped her bundle and applied herself to the double portrait. It was fixed at each corner with a pair of screws. Lionel watched the child-sized fingers at work. They nimbly removed the lower left screws, followed by the top right. Lionel opened his palm for them. She had the short, straight hair of a mediaeval pageboy. The front locks swung across her jaw. Refocussing on the lower right screws, she began to giggle. "This one's bewitched. It keeps slipping."

Lionel watched, stagey and unperturbed. He wondered how her hair could be so glossy. Then she gave a yelp, withdrawing from the wall while still supporting the picture. "Oh yuck," she exclaimed. "I've injured myself."

"Just don't injure the painting," Lionel replied heartlessly. Blood was running from her thumb. She found a handkerchief and wound it round. Lionel made a motion towards the door. There was Sylvia, pale as a ghost. He went over to her, doubly dismayed. "I was about to fetch plaster for a cut finger."

"I'll get it," Sylvia said.

Lionel returned to the portrait. The screwdriver was passed to him with the suggestion that he should finish the job.

Lionel carefully placed the screws he had been holding on the mantlepiece. Then he addressed himself to the lower right screws. His visitor prowled round the summer parlour, commenting on the tapestries. Lionel glanced up. "Just hold it in place a minute, could you?" With that, he hurried to the door. There was no sign of Sylvia. "I won't be a jiffy," he called, and went in search. They met on the landing outside Sylvia's bedroom. Lionel took the box of plaster and guided her towards the kitchen. "Stay in there and get Annie to make you some tea," he urged. "You would have been better at the Lodge. As we all agreed. Why martyr yourself by coming up now?"

Sylvia obeyed, with slow steps. She halted at the door. "Please think again!" she implored.

Lionel shook his head, lifted his hand and ran up the turnpike to the summer parlour. Once there, he stood guard on the picture while the plaster was applied. Then he gave Miss Hardie his most engaging smile. "I think you should do the honours," he stated. "I will hold it firm."

But Miss Hardie declined, laughing diffidently. It was Lionel who removed the final screws, while the girl steadied the picture. After this successful ceremony she wrapped it first in a length of cotton sheet, then in a blanket. Lionel carried it to the front door. Of Sylvia there was no sign. He laid the Rossetti in the boot of the car and closed the lid. The lid of the coffin, he silently observed. He shook the tiny undamaged hand. "There's a good place in Crossways, if you want some lunch." He clapped the door to. Waving the car away, he did not notice the pallid face staring from an upstairs window, witness to the painting's departure.

Sylvia dreamt that night that Drummond was with her at Penwhapple. Gradually he descended the turnpike stair. Sylvia sensed he was not in the castle any more but on the path to the burn. Above her, on the turret, she could hear a dog barking, then the toll of the Penwhapple bell.

"He stepping down by zig-zag paths and juts of pointed rock,
Came on the shining levels of the lake."

She woke, damp with sweat. It was early morning. She had seen the double portrait being taken away. The heart of the castle was gone. She got up. As soon as she felt it was reasonable to intrude on Gwen's routine she drove to Ayr.

Drummond had had a good night. A new oxygen cylinder was to be delivered that afternoon. Gwen confided in Sylvia that she hoped to get Drummond through at least until Christmas. "I take everything a step at a time now."

Sylvia sat with her brother while Gwen took the dog round the block. He mentioned the arrangement he had made for Tiffany in his Will. "I haven't told that one yet," he said, meaning Gwen. Sylvia was shocked by his behaviour. As soon as she got back to Penwhapple she telephoned Ogier about the trees.

At the weekend the school van rolled up at the castle, with Ogier, Pat and a well-equipped detachment of Somersby volunteers. While Annie served the youngsters hot drinks and biscuits, Sylvia, Ogier and Pat reconnoitred the positions in which Sylvia had decided the trees should be planted. Ogier and Pat then set up two working parties. Ogier's, the larger, prepared the ground. Pat's planted out. Phoebe and Robert were placed in separate groups. Otherwise there was no conscious attempt at segregation. Sylvia directed operations in her lethal rubber boots. At midday there still seemed an enormous amount to do. But by the time Annie offered tea in the banqueting hall everything was planted. Eighty-six trees and shrubs in all, according to Pat. There was a happy atmosphere in the castle, a great fire in the library and a guided tour, which Sylvia found it necessary to cut a bit short. In Bryony's day, she felt, children would not have made silly jokes all the time. The planting, she decided, was going to be a great success. The black mulberry had been reserved for Gwen. It might just fruit one day in the Dower House garden.

That night Drummond died in Gwen's arms. He had told her he would feel safe that way, and Gwen received much credit for being there as Drummond had wanted. She kept remembering how Drummond had lain along the bed, his tongue rising stiffly and falling slackly, without semblance of speech or conscious effort.

Drummond's Memorial Service was held in Holy Trinity. There was some dissent about this, because the Penwhapple connection was with Old Dailly. They deferred to Gwen, who had nursed Drummond through his final illness, and who had preferred the more substantial city church. She sat in the place of honour in the front pew. As Tiffany squeezed past to read the second lesson, Gwen surreptitiously passed her a tiny square of lacy lawn. With it Tiffany, equally surreptitiously, wiped her nose. She was wearing a sensational black hat.

The first lesson had been read by Lionel. Ecclesiastes 3, verses 1 to 15, "To everything there is a season." Lionel spoke it with relish.

"A time to love, and a time to hate; a time of war, and a time of peace."

He wore the Penwhapple tweed. Because he was so much slighter than Drummond, and of fairer colouring, the faded lovat made him look almost transparent.

As the mourners filed out after the service, Stewart Urquhart stopped for a word. A satisfactory price for the Rossetti had been agreed. "I appreciate that the point of this exercise is to enable the family to keep everything together," he murmured. "But if you change your mind about leasing, and I really think you may have to, our experience is that the separate sale of house and contents is almost always more satisfactory." He began to waddle away, then swung the padded shelf of his posterior in a jaunty half circle. "We could advise you if you decide to go ahead."

Much the best plan, thought Lionel, with a disturbing sense of euphoria. Sylvia and Iona were busy fielding a separate queue of sympathisers. Of Ricky there was no sign. Tiffany had remained in the kirk, blubbing showily in the family pew. It was time to disperse. He was the eleventh Laird now. He had removed Penwhapple's double portrait from the wall, and survived.

Chapter 14

"When siblings start to die, it's the beginning of the end." Seated in Iona's front room, Sylvia implied it was a pity the family had disregarded her warning over the double portrait, but, seeing they had, she would enjoy watching them take the consequences. It was sad about Drummond. Now Iona was not looking too good either. "If only Tiffany could have stayed longer," she said. "She would have enjoyed Ogier's performance in the Christmas play."

Iona's concern was for Sylvia. "Why don't you sleep in her bed tonight?" she asked. "I can lend you a nightie. You know where things are."

"I think I might. We could have that goat's cheese you won't let me pay for."

Iona's concern changed into amusement. It was typical of Sylvia to stay on the pretext of sharing a piece of goat's cheese. "That's settled then. I agree that Tiffany would have enjoyed Ogier as King Herod. Most amusing. And little Pippa Cursiter as the Angel! She really was angelic."

"Yes, it's always the trouble-makers who are the best angels. They seem to grasp the possibilities unerringly. When does Tiffany get back?"

"At the weekend, provided the weather doesn't interfere. I intend to spoil her. She has been so dreadfully upset by Drummond's death."

"You're the one who needs spoiling. I shall tell her so."

"Please don't. Tiffany can be such an organising person. Now, what do you say to an aubergine bobotie? We could try the goat's cheese in it. Or shall we just have the cheese with some wholemeal bread?"

Sylvia decided that bobotie would be more festive than just bread. Bobotie was also a good deal more trouble, and Iona was fussed because she had no peas to give it colour. She was surprised that Sylvia had not chosen the simpler meal.

Sylvia said, "I'm not happy about the money, Iona."

They were finishing coffee and Iona was wondering if she should put on the news. "What money?" she asked, her mind on the petty cash they had worked out with traditional exactitude not two hours earlier.

"The money!" Sylvia insisted. "My share of the estate. On my death I want it to go to Ricky and Tiffany. I had thought of making Tiffany my sole heir, seeing that Ricky will do quite well with the family business. But what about Ogier? All that money we're getting for the family portrait. Perhaps I should leave some to Ogier?"

Iona was at a loss. Sylvia had not looked at her while speaking. She addressed the dark spaces of the French doors, a slight frown between her eyes. Iona got up and pulled the curtains across, as though to defend her sister. She said, "But why Ogier? Ogier is probably better off than we are, with all our commitments."

"Ogier can't have that much. The school pays next to nothing, in fact he gets less than Ricky. Tell me honestly, what do you think? It's never too late to alter one's Will."

"But why? Why feel it necessary? I don't think it would be appropriate at all. Ogier has the school. It provides him with a very good way of life, one he has chosen. I'm sure he wouldn't welcome any drastic change in his favour. He'd be most embarrassed."

"Then there's something else. The picture."

"The picture?" It was like a silly game.

"Sholto's drawing of the original Fogo. It always belonged to the school. The school must have it back."

"You mean that caricature in charcoal?"

"Brown wash, heightened with white. We had such laughs over that picture, Ant and I. We used to say Fogo was waiting to bark." Sylvia smiled introspectively. "It's a good picture for children. It gives them faith in the animal kingdom. Drummond would say it should go back."

"I don't suppose Drummond ever gave it a thought. But if you feel so strongly about it, the picture had better be returned."

"It meant something special to me when I was in the College of Teachers. Ogier understood that, and made me have it in the castle." Sylvia looked at Iona. "You forget one thing. Suppose Ogier wanted to marry. He would need money then. I want him to have my share of the money for the Rossetti, Iona, I've quite decided."

"Come now, Sylvia. This is make-believe. We'll talk about it tomorrow morning."

Very soon after this exchange, Sylvia went to bed. Iona followed. All that fuss over a rather ugly cartoon was worrying enough. But, surely, the money from the Rossetti was not Sylvia's to give! It was needed for up-grading Penwhapple. Only then did Iona realise that Sylvia was not deceived. She realised perfectly well what Iona, too, had known in her heart all along. There was no intention on anyone's part that a penny should go on the castle. The money from the Rossetti would be shared out amongst the family, to spend as they liked. It was an agreeable prospect.

It occurred to Iona that perhaps Sylvia was being devious. Was it conceivable that she saw Ogier installed there with Pippa? Thc idea was so improbable that Iona felt better. She fell asleep, sure that everything would be clear in the morning.

There was a heavy fall of snow at the weekend, through which Tiffany had had to drive. Pleased with her adventure – she had taken the motorway and avoided the worst-hit areas - she celebrated by taking all the bathwater and helping herself to Iona's bath oil. Then she announced she was going to see Pippa at Somersby, instead of making a duty visit to Gwen, as Iona thought they had agreed. She was glad to see the back of her daughter.

"How's your campaign against Samantha going?" Tiffany collapsed onto Pippa's bed, ramming a cushion behind her.

"I get on quite well with Samantha now. The tension is between her and Ogier. We're not supposed to breathe a word of what happens at College meetings, so don't pass this on, will you? But Sam is still pushing the idea of moving Somersby into Ayr. It would attract more day-pupils there, of course. Sam dresses it up, as you can imagine. We have to make The Education more widely available, that sort of stuff."

"And whose side are you on?"

"Ogier's! He's quite prepared to start a school in Ayr, but not to wind up everything here. Mind you, I think the future does lie with Somersby becoming a day school."

"What about you and Ogier? Any advances?" Tiffany raised

her arms to adjust the cushion. "Have you got him into bed yet?"

Pippa tossed her head. "You know full well it's not like that. Perhaps I respect Ogier too much."

"Perhaps he's indifferent?"

Her words stung. "Possibly. Though not probably. I think you'd be quite surprised at how much I'm able to contribute to the school now."

"Do you not have something of a father fixation, Pippa? You'll never find anyone good enough if so."

"Because I happen to find older men more interesting? Unlike you with your juveniles."

"Ricky?"

"Well of course, there's always Ricky"

Unruffled, Tiffany considered. "Ricky's a poppet. He's so uncomplicated. That's what appeals to me. I so enjoy dominating him!"

It was disconcerting to have one's confidences met with such detachment. Pippa said, "I believe I am sort of in love with Ogier. Ricky, as you say, is somewhat obvious."

"I take it Ricky has renewed his attentions, then?"

"Let's just say I'm not interested. He inveigled me to one of those awful Christmas parties in town, at the end of last term. We had just been doing the Kings' Play. The contrast was too much. I made him bring me home early. I know what you mean about dominating him. He minds so much but tries not to let you know."

"Pippa, you're a disgrace. You're a cock-tease, do you know that?"

"What a revolting thing to say. You, who've never slept with a man in your life."

"I will, though. Sexy lights and music and a bolt on the bedroom door!" Tiffany gave her friend another appraising look. Was Pippa rather afraid of nudity and sex? "Being in love with a father figure would inhibit you, I imagine?" Tiffany asked. "Make you concentrate on the beloved's mind. But whatever your feelings, don't exploit Ogier's, will you Pip?"

It occurred to Pippa that Tiffany's feelings for Ogier were more proprietorial than she knew. As though effecting a more adult change of key, she sat forward, saying, "Ogier has a male certainty about everything. His comments on Tennyson, for example, can be so dogmatic they're absurd." She went to rummage in a drawer, taking out a file and beginning, with great precision, to trim her nails. "He spends far too much time in the past." Pippa spoke more amicably, as though inviting debate.

Tiffany shook her head. "I would have said the opposite."

Pippa held out a hand and tilted it to the light. "As far as I'm concerned, education has to prepare children for the present." She began using a transparent nail varnish.

"There is a really nice side of Ricky," said Tiffany. "Uncle Drummond blatantly favouritised me. Ricky never let it bother him. Perhaps I ought to marry him after all!"

"Now that really is nonsense! Ricky's treated like the Prodigal Son in your family. Besides, cousins shouldn't marry. There's enough oddness already."

Tiffany jumped up. "You wouldn't come to the Dower House with me, would you? I promised Mum I'd go. It's partly to do with that business of the Sangrail I told you about. They haven't got probate yet, so no-one is supposed to know anything about it, but of course they do, and according to Mum the Sangrail has disappeared. So I'm supposed to go along and comment tactfully. Can you imagine anything more horrendous? Aunt Sylvia wants to talk to me too - something about her Will, I gather. It's so off-putting that I haven't been to see her either. So. Can you come to Ayr with me? We could look up Ricky, if you're good."

"I can come if we're back by six. If you want to see Ricky, count me out."

"I've got to be back by six myself. Evening with Mum, special dish she and Sylvia have invented. She'll want to talk. With all this snow I'll have to set off in good time tomorrow."

Returning to the Dower House, Gwen felt old. That afternoon she had found herself noting the phenomenon of youth, abundantly evident on the streets of Ayr. Active young men with straight backs and flat stomachs. Supple girls. Their ability to read minuscule print in shops and offices, without spectacles. In the isolation of her home Gwen succumbed to melancholic nostalgia. The conservatory was still filled with the geraniums which Drummond had brought in during his last, brief remission. Something caught her eye. It was the expanding dog-lead, hanging from a coat hook. She took it down without expression.

"Everything is hatefully dirty," she said, surveying carpets and furniture. "I wish I could feel it still mattered." Tears of grief welled up. But it was a strange grief, mixed with the bleakest sense of betrayal. Drummond had let her down, giving in to death before Christmas.

When the bell sounded it turned out to be Tiffany and her friend from Somersby. Gwen had the measure of Pippa. For Tiffany she allowed herself a surge of outrage. What had Drummond meant to her beyond a welcoming smile and kind words? Tiffany had let months go by, without bothering to write or come up. She had abused her special place in Drummond's heart. He had left her a portion of their married life in his desk and those bits of pottery. A more than splendid reward for consenting to be the beloved niece.

"May we come in?"

"Of course. I was just about to make tea. No. Let's all have a drink." A bit early, but so much easier than boiling a kettle. It would be about the vases that Tiffany had come.

"We'll only stay half an hour or so. Mum expects me home early, and Pippa has evening duty at the Mansion. Nothing for me, please. I'm driving."

"How is your mother? Is she eating better now? If only she wasn't such a rigid vegetarian. That must be a worry for you."

"She's definitely lost weight. But we're having one of her specials tonight, something she and Aunt Sylvia have invented."

Gwen poured them all a drink, disregarding the fact that Tiffany did not want one. They discussed the advantages and disadvantages of vegetarian cookery, Pippa coming out more strongly in support than Tiffany. Gwen said, "Your mother was telling me how much Sylvia has declined. I know that Andrew Schofield is quite shocked."

"Mother is worried because of Aunt Sylvia's strange moods. She thinks her illness is psychological. It started when the picture went."

Gwen nodded. "I remember how sad Sylvia was when we first discussed the matter. It seems a long time ago now. But, you know, your aunt was influenced by sentiment, not reason. If you remember that, Tiffany, you will feel less upset about her."

"How are you bearing up, Gwen?" Tiffany's question was rather too guileless. She looked around the room. It required an effort not to seek the lost Sangrail, or verify the other pieces. "Where's Fogo?" He was usually energetically in their midst, or barking in protest from the kitchen.

Gwen did not hesitate. "I had him put down." She looked Tiffany steadily in the eye.

Tiffany turned to Pippa and back to Gwen. "What was wrong with him?"

"He was Drummond's dog, never mine. He'd had a good life. I didn't care to see him growing older."

"But he was so fit! Did Uncle Drummond want you to put him down?"

"I certainly didn't say anything to Drummond. But he would have understood what was best." Gwen spoke with calm sincerity.

Tiffany gazed about the room rather wildly. "Darling Fogo. But I do realise how much he'd have missed Drummond."

"Won't you finish that drink, Tiffany? A top-up for you, Pippa?" Gwen advanced with the bottle.

Tiffany stood, obliging Pippa to stand too. "We mustn't impose on you." Gwen saw them to the door. "Mother hopes you'll have dinner with her next week," Tiffany forced herself to say. "She'll give you a ring."

"It was sweet of you to come. Tell Iona I'm coping well and look forward to seeing her. I've promised to visit Sylvia on Monday. I may look in then."

"Coping well!" Tiffany exploded as they drove out of Ayr. "She's murdered my uncle's dog. There's always been a Fogo in the family. I'll never trust her again."

"Then why on earth didn't you ask about the Sangrail?"

"I know. I should have demanded it. But it would have seemed grasping, when we're still awaiting probate. In any case, I didn't trust myself to speak." Tiffany could not bring herself to tell Pippa that the Sangrail did, indeed, appear to be missing. Nor did she find it possible to unburden herself to Iona that evening. She turned her mother's cautious questions aside.

Chapter 15

"I'm surprised Pippa feels she must contribute so much." Samantha lost no time in squaring up to Ogier. "The meeting would have ended half an hour ago if we had not had to listen to her holding forth."

"I stand rebuked."

"Oh, you're not responsible for Pippa's every fault. She must learn to be more succinct, that's all. Forgive me for saying this, Ogier, but I have been put in a completely false position with the Education Department by the way you summarised our discussion this evening."

"Sam, I say again, there is no objection to a pioneering initiative in Ayr. Provided it is not at the expense of all we have achieved here."

"Would you cut off discussion quite so firmly if it was Pippa who was talking? You could see for yourself that opinion was more divided than you allow."

"Look, I intended no irony when I accepted your rebuke about Pippa. But I think you owe me an apology on the Ayr business. Of course I know the College is divided. That is why it was wrong of you to approach the Department without telling me. Support for the school will be undermined if the parents start hearing rumours."

"Well, I won't reopen the discussion. But there are several families which would support a move to town. As for Pippa, I think some of the work she is doing, especially with the Highers English group, is very promising."

"Yes, but she should intervene less at College meetings. I expect I've been too patient."

"Could you be patient one more moment with me then? I just wanted to ask you - is there any chance the Dower House could be converted into a school? Supposing Gwen was happy to leave."

"The Dower House?" Ogier shook his head. "Well, that's an unlikely scenario. However, you've mentioned the idea now, so let me reflect." A sense of weariness overcame him. "It would be damaging if you and I, of all people, no longer understood one another, Sam. You are such a pillar of strength."

A pillar of salt, Samantha told herself, thinking that Ogier little understood the resentment she felt. The idea of supplanting Ogier as Chairman of the College of Teachers insinuated itself, not for the first time. She would tell the Local Education Department that she had exceeded her authority. And she would suppress her antagonism towards Pippa.

Ogier returned to his office. He regretted the confrontation with Samantha, the climate of rancour and ill-will. If it reflected on his chairmanship, he had better consider making way for someone new. Time passed. He ceased to think, but drifted on a current of reflections. It was comfortable in his old leather chair. He had indeed let Pippa hold forth too much. Closing his eyes, he recalled the kneeling knight in Before the Battle, the gaze of adoration which Phoebe had seen in the picture; amidst the fatigue of conflict, a youthful gaze remaining constant, evoking the concentration he so admired in Pippas' face. In his imagination, the forms merged. Dark, anonymous, lurid shapes circled round. Gradually he brought Pippa closer until she was swathed in light. Then she was triumphantly unclad, standing within an arm's length, softly curved and white, and he naked, kneeling at her feet. He watched himself stand and draw her against him.

The telephone shattered his reverie. "I am so glad to catch you. Can you possibly come to the castle?" It was Iona. "Sylvia will not be able to rest until she knows you are here. Dear Ogier. Prepare yourself. She may not be able to speak to you, may not even know who you are. But it is you she wants. Please come as quickly as you can."

Ogier ran down to his utilitarian old car as if to a fully caparisoned destrier, acutely aware that ahead of him, at the castle, a spirit was in crisis. He drove up the track without heed for potholes, composing his own spirit to assist in the release of Sylvia's. Between the Somersby lane and Penwhapple gates he repeated, inwardly,

Strive, heart, and bear, joyful, the light
Into the world of winter night.
Strike, seedling in the winter ground.
Let God's voice, creative, sound.

Moments later he was through the front door. Iona was on the landing. She tried to speak and had no voice. Ogier gripped her hand. They went down the passage to Sylvia's bedroom. In the doorway Iona managed to whisper huskily, "She's barely with us. She may not know you." As Ogier started forward Iona pulled him back, whispering, "Dr Schofield is on his way."

Ogier nodded. He lost no further time. Sylvia lay propped on two embroidered pillows, her eyes open. He sat quickly and quietly beside her, laying a hand on the quilt. It was cold in the room. Sylvia's eyes very slowly moved to focus on Ogier. He leaned nearer. "She telephoned this evening to say she was feeling unwell. Luckily I hadn't gone to bed," Iona muttered by his ear, as if excusing herself. He scarcely took in her words, so intent was he on communicating with the dying woman.

Her eyes seemed devoid of light and understanding. Confident nevertheless that she recognised him, Ogier spoke her name very softly, half smiling, assuring her that all was well. She made no sound. Ogier hung on to his sense that she was with him. Iona, who had gone to the window, returned to the bedside. After what seemed a long time they heard cars prowling down the drive. In a moment Andrew Schofield was by the bed. Lionel appeared. Ogier withdrew to let the doctor come near. He nodded at Lionel, who followed Andrew towards the bed.

The doctor looked round. "I'm afraid she's slipped away," he said.

Ogier felt his own heart fail. She had crossed the threshold, even as he had removed himself from her side.

Chapter 16

Ogier returned to Somersby soon after dawn, and almost immediately found himself swept up in school business. One of his earlier appointments was with Pippa, whom he had agreed to see during the morning break. Once again the problem was Robert and, once again, Pippa had worked herself into a state of moral indignation. This time what Robert had done sounded more problematic than his usual misdemeanours. Phoebe Donaldson had been involved. Ogier was inclined to think that she rather than Robert might have precipitated things.

When Pippa came to the office door a minute or so early, she appeared chastened to the point of nervousness. Without quite looking at Ogier she was intensely aware that his face had suddenly become old and drawn. She avoided the comfortable chair and sat well forward on an upright Edinburgh chair near his desk.

"Now. Tell me again exactly what happened."

Pippa made herself meet his eye. "I'm terribly sorry about Sylvia's death, Ogier. And you were with her, I understand."

"Yes. I'd somehow expected her to live to be a hundred."

"You must be exhausted."

"Surprisingly, no. In a strange way, I'm reinforced by Sylvia's courage."

"That's wonderful."

"Come on now. Let's tease out this problem before you have to join a class."

She felt the reluctance to share his grief as a rebuke. "I'm afraid I was knocked off balance, Ogier. I'm sorry. I don't think I handled things at all well. I let them see I was upset and a bit fazed."

"Listen, Pippa, I'm sure we mustn't over-react. Find an opportunity to take Phoebe aside. Talk to her on a personal level, as if you were her older sister. Tell her that when the time comes to have a physical relationship it won't be something to rush into. Encourage her to talk to her mother in the holidays. That should help her understand her feelings better."

"Some of the older girls make it quite clear they'll take their time to start a family. If they have one at all. There's plenty of that sort of talk."

"It's tricky. One doesn't want to push the idea of protection. But I'm impressed. Phoebe seems to have been reasonably open with you. That at least is positive."

There was a pause. Ogier's reference to protection struck Pippa as pretty cool. "I'll certainly talk to Phoebe," she said. "But what about Robert?"

"Leave Robert to me."

He went to a tray with cups and a coffee pot, saying "You'll need this as much as I do," and then poured the coffee without asking Pippa how she liked it. He drank his gazing out of the window. Giving a start, he offered her the plate of biscuits, taking two for himself.

She blurted out, "I'm sorry to be throwing this problem at you, when something so really awful had happened."

"Sad, yes, but not awful." Ogier's smile took her aback. "Wholly natural. As natural as the young wanting to discover themselves."

"I hope Sylvia didn't die because she was unhappy." Pippa longed to be taken into his confidence.

"Unhappy? No, Sylvia wasn't given to being unhappy. She was a sensible, positive person." Musing a little, he observed more hesitantly, "I fear that's not quite true. She became deeply unhappy after her brother's death. She began to worry about material possessions, at the very time when she should have been letting go. But peace was with her last night. That is why I can honestly say I drew strength from her death. I hope you will not think me morbid. My feelings are truly the opposite to that." He stood up.

Pippa stood also. She placed her cup on the tray.

"Don't go yet," Ogier said urgently. He felt far removed, displaced, in several worlds at once. On one level he was held by a vision of two youngsters drawn together in sensual need, on another by the memory of an old spinster lying alone in the Penwhapple state bed. As though forcing himself from Sylvia's presence he caught Pippa's shoulders, pulling her towards him, inhaling deeply, keeping her bound against him. He lowered his head at an angle and, with deliberation, set his mouth over her mouth.

He was not prepared for her reaction. She stepped backwards and spoke quietly. "Ogier? Are you ill?" The greenish eyes were cool, the brows unclouded. Very slightly she tilted her childish, lovely nose at him.

His lips had been on hers. He longed for the chance to prove what he was, what he felt, how infinite his physical power could be. He spoke in a strong, happy voice. "Pippa, I can't disguise my feelings for you. I love you, I admire you, I desire you. Possibly I am ill. But only with the pleasure of telling you the truth, darling girl." He tried to draw her towards him again.

"This is rather confusing." Pippa, agitated and excited, and precariously tempted to yield up every charm and weapon she possessed, nevertheless held aloof. "The educationalist one moment, then suddenly . . . this." She was genuinely at a loss, his timing was so unexpected.

Ogier took Pippa's hand and pressed it to his lips. "Pippa, don't wound me," he begged. "I want you to know, with the deepest truth of my heart, I love you." Again he raised arms to embrace her.

She went closer to him, catching his hands and pressing them against her breast, her heart beating extravagantly. Her admiration for Ogier had developed into a powerful affection. She had encouraged it, whatever Tiffany had been assured to the contrary. But Pippa was sufficiently in awe of death to be mindful of Sylvia's passing. Momentarily she saw her young powers in a modified perspective. Then there was Ricky. His presence in her thoughts exercised a still stronger influence, whatever Tiffany had been told. Lifting her face, she kissed Ogier, her eyes never leaving his. A little nerve in his eyelid was flickering slightly. "I can't help doubting whether you are quite yourself, Ogier," she murmured. "I never want you to regret anything which happens between us now."

A numbing agent was indeed lifting from him, exposing every nerve to pain and embarrassment. He was dismayed to the point of disgust at having expressed himself so rashly. Strong emotions long banked down. "I expect you would consider me too old," he said, desperately seeking a truth less hurtful.

She said, "I love you, Ogier." Then she by no means comforted him by adding, "But that is all. You are not too old for me. I like looking up to you, respecting you. The truth is, I just hadn't thought of us in a physical sense."

Divided between declaring and excusing himself, Ogier gave a short laugh. "You might be surprised if you knew me better. I have been discovering a whole new dimension in myself since knowing you, Pippa."

She had contrived just such a scene in her imagination more than once, with varying results. But the shade of Sylvia had never before presided. Nor had she been upstaged by teen-age sex. Their hands came apart. "I must go now. I have to prepare for my next class."

She took her time opening the door and passing through it. Ogier, watching her, had never felt so mortified. He stood like a man who had contaminated his soul.

Chapter 17

A Festival of Remembrance was held for Sylvia during the Easter holidays. It was a warm day, bright with Spring sunshine. Camelot was packed. There was a sizable contingent from the East Coast. Friends who had not seen Sylvia for years had made the journey to Ayrshire. Tiffany was not the only one to have travelled all the way from London.

Ogier introduced the afternoon's proceedings, speaking with clumsy intensity.

"Dear Friends. Sylvia Moffat died early this year, in the Season of the Epiphany, when the wise of the world seek spiritual revelation. In death she joined herself to this quest. We now remember her at Easter, surrounded by images of Parsifal, whose legend was so dear to Sylvia's heart. But it is another favourite story of Sylvia's that I want to share with you today. As you know, every year since Somersby was founded, we have performed a Christmas play. This year it was the most difficult of these plays, known as the Three King's Play. In it the Wise Men seek Christ's cradle, guided by the soft shining of the Star of Grace."

Here there was an irresolute pause.

Ogier resumed, "Caspar, Melchior and Balthazar are true kings. But we must remember that the play contains a fourth king, King Herod. I acted that part myself this year, to Sylvia's amusement. Villains are much the easiest to play."

Ogier paused again, smiling now.

"King Herod is always with us. Sylvia used to say he was in the Covetous King of Merlin's prophecy, the foreign usurper whom Robert the Bruce drove from Scottish soil. But Sylvia was thinking of something more important than short-lived, worldly triumph. For her, the crucial battle is with the Covetous King whom we all carry inside ourselves. Our task is to transform King Herod into a companion fit to join the spiritual pilgrimage of the Wise. My dear friends, it is in this way that we can not only remember Sylvia, but help her – now. Yes. So be it."

A further pause, then Ogier spoke in a lighter vein.

"This," he concluded, "is a family occasion. By that I mean an occasion for everyone whom Sylvia included in her extensive circle of friends, colleagues and pupils. We begin our Festival of Remembrance with a contribution from Sylvia's niece, Tiffany Ramsay. Tiffany, you are going to read us an extract from The Bridal of Triermain?"

"Yes'" said Tiffany, coming forward. "I am going to read a series of extracts which I know Aunt Sylvia would have enjoyed." She arranged her notes on the lectern and looked up at the audience. "But let me explain why I have chosen Sir Walter Scott's poem. The founder of Somersby, Bryony Moffat, painted a picture inspired by it. Quotations from the poem are inscribed all over the castle. Aunt Sylvia loved the picture, and the poem. My first extract I am sure will have inspired Sholto Moffat, when he courageously undertook the remodelling of the family stronghold."

Tiffany embarked on her reading with Scott's description of the Castle of Saint John. Some of the extracts which followed were unexpectedly cheerful, others a litany of splendid names. She ended with a passage which, she felt, particularly evoked her aunt.

> "We will love them yet,
> The mountain's misty coronet,
> The greenwood, and the wold;
> And love the more, that of their maze
> Adventure high of other days
> By ancient bards is told,
> Bringing, perchance, like my poor tale,
> Some moral truth in fiction's veil;
> Nor love them less, that o'er the hill
> The evening breeze, as now, comes chill."

She closed her notes and looked up. "And now I am about to be upstaged by my Cousin Ricky. Aunt Sylvia always called Ricky and me the Heavenly Twins. We were great rivals for her affection. I remember when we devised a test for her. Who would she save, if we both fell into a pool of crocodiles? I must say she was a most unsatisfactory aunt. She never gave us a straight answer. Dear friends, Ricky."

"Right," said Ricky mounting the podium with studied informality. "I am not going to compete with all this literary stuff. Naturally my eccentric old aunt loved Tiffany best. I'll just do what I've always done and trail along in her wake. I'm going to read a short chapter from the Bible, the one Tiffany read at our Uncle Drummond's Memorial Service. I know Aunt Sylvia liked it very much." And he proceeded to read 1 Corinthians, Chapter 13, in the authorised version, Faith, Hope and Charity.

The afternoon continued with music and readings, punctuated by short appreciations from friends and colleagues. Ogier had little more to do. Each contributor was primed to introduce the next. Yet again he found himself examining his feelings for Pippa. He was touched by her hesitations. He delighted in her tendency to dramatise herself. But already she was recreating the truth about their friendship. She loved him, that was all! He had behaved foolishly. He seemed to hear Sylvia's voice: "Not Somersby material at all."

Deep in his heart, Ogier took issue with Sylvia. He was prepared to champion Pippa against all the odds. As if in a trance he stood and heard himself saying, "I must now bring our afternoon to a close. There will be tea in the Mansion. I hope as many of you as possible will stay. But first we will join in singing the School Song, so beloved of Sylvia."

Everyone stood to sing.

In the Mansion Lionel took Gwen a cup of tea and asked her what she had thought of Ogier's "presentation."

"When he started talking about King Herod I really and truly expected you to take a bow, Lionel."

Lionel laughed. "And Tiffany? All that literary stuff, as Ricky called it?"

"Tiffany is Tiffany. But such self-confidence! The young people were splendid. You must be proud of Ricky. Please tell him so - for your own sake, Lionel, as much as his."

"My dear Gwen, I am a great fan of Ricky's. I need to temper my feelings. Perish the notion I should gush! But as a matter of fact

I thought he acquitted himself pretty well. I am not as grudging as you think."

"Having Tiffany home for a while will be good for Iona."

"Yes, my dear sister has been behaving rather oddly. Look at her now, hurrying about with a teapot. Who on earth is that strange character she is talking to, as if he were Royalty?" The strange character wore overalls tucked into his socks, and had shoulder-length, wavy hair. It was Hal Hogarth, the man against whom all charges had been dropped.

"I haven't the slightest idea," said Gwen.

"You know, these two rooms could easily be reinstated. I'm not sure if the school knocked them into one, or if they were originally divided by double doors. Everything is intact. The cornice, the fireplaces, the original shutters. And have you seen the old panelling in Ogier's study upstairs? A real gem. Bring the farm back in hand and I could imagine Ricky installed here. Knock down the Victorian wing, of course, and put all those ghastly rabbit hutches to the torch."

"And you'd keep an eye on him from the castle, I suppose."

"I still feel we ought to lease the castle. But my idea now is we should sell the contents first. Good Lord, speak of the devil. It's those Canadians I wanted you to meet."

"What an adorable girl Tiffany Ramsay is," Josephine Feinstein was saying to Samantha. "She has superstar quality. Tell me about her. I'm sure I've seen her before."

"She floats through life, does Miss Ramsay. She was a student here, as you may have gathered. She did well at Saint Andrew's, worked briefly for a newspaper and then picked up a job as press officer at the Scottish Office. You may have seen her on television, hovering in the background. She's photogenic, and very ambitious."

"What say we ask her to model for us?" said Gloria. "We're into photography, you know. We'd just love to take some photographs of the school for you, perhaps with Tiffany revisiting her old classroom and dreaming about life's great changes."

"That deep voice of hers!" said Josephine. "Would that be a West Side accent?"

Samantha became aware that Lionel was hovering. "You must let me introduce you to the Chairman of our Trustees," she said. "Mr Lionel Moffat. And his sister-in-law, Gwen Moffat."

"But of course we know Mr Moffat. That was a wonderful service for your sister, Mr Moffat. Just how we remember her, wasn't it, Jo?"

"How kind of you to support the occasion."

"We felt we knew her, Mr Moffat. We felt there was a bond. And your son! He was fine. You must tell him he was the most adorable thing of the whole afternoon."

"Adorable. Very well, I will tell him that. Now, I particularly want you to talk to my sister-in-law, my late brother's widow." Smoothly, Lionel brought Gwen forward. "She will be able to give you a more objective opinion of the castle than I could. I'm far too attached to the place. We will be working up proposals for a proper lease, without all those complications which I know you found unappealing. Perhaps you will be putting down tartan carpets after all, Miss Lance. The contents of the castle, incidentally, are probably going to be auctioned this autumn. You and Miss Feinstein must attend the sale. It will be of far more than local interest."

Josephine subjected Gwen to the careful scrutiny she reserved for very feminine, older women. Lionel slipped off, having business to discuss with Samantha. He sensed the tension between her and Ogier and had decided to play cat and mouse with them. His first move would be to make difficulties over the next Trustee meeting.

He must act at once if an auction of the contents of Penwhapple was indeed to take place. Iona was still dithering. He had better speak to her before Tiffany disappeared to London. It was a great pity the younger generation now had a say in what should happen. On the other hand, they could hardly prove less manageable than Sylvia. They must be swept along before they realised the power they had. Part cryptic, part gleeful, Lionel saw Ogier talking to the man in the woollen hat. Having dropped his poison in Samantha's ear he found himself having to listen to one of her lectures about Somersby. A single issue person, Miss Spencer.

Stoically smiling, Lionel heard her out.

Chapter 18

Lionel arrived at Iona's as she and Tiffany were finishing their evening meal. He loitered in the living room while they tidied up, drawn to Iona's desk like a carrion crow to tidbits. "Just rummaging through your papers,' he assured her, as she returned to the room. "I always loved your youthful diaries." Settling on the settee, he informed her that he had something to say "before Tiffany bursts in." He enjoyed his sister's unease at this remark.

"I know how upset you are by Sylvia's death," he told her. "The rites of passage at Somersby will have helped, I hope. But you have been overdoing it. There was no need to sort out Sylvia's belongings as if new tenants were chasing you. And there's no need to keep going up to the castle now." He allowed his air of gravitas to be subverted by a small, involuntary smirk.

"I cannot bear clutter. And I simply could not bear the thought of strangers going through Sylvia's most personal belongings."

"Look at it this way. She has been spared the disruption of a move. We remember her as our indomitable sister and a remarkable woman. We can now take a more rational approach to the castle. Have you thought about my proposal? If we are to auction the contents we must instruct Stewart Urquhart very soon. We must not let Penwhapple stand empty over the winter. We certainly do not have time for another stately gavotte with the Museum."

"I begin to agree with you. The whole lot to go. Everything auctioned."

Lionel drummed his fingers on one of the occasional tables. "Stewart advises that we could expect a minimum of fifty thousand pounds each, possibly twice as much. That will be a nice little sum to add to what we are getting for the Rossetti. You are not to know this, but there was a last minute suggestion from the Museum that they should pay for that by instalments. Stewart put them right. I thought it best not to worry you with hypothetical problems. Anyway, the money is now coming through. You look troubled."

"No. Not about that."

"What, then?"

Iona asked herself yet again if she should tell Lionel about Sylvia's wish to leave her interest in the Rossetti to Ogier. "Nothing," she said. There was no point. Lionel would not countenance the idea, even if she could bring herself to prejudice Tiffany's interests by telling him. She shook her head. It was no use even mentioning Ogier's name. "And Ogier?" she tentatively asked.

"Blow Ogier. He has no say in what we do. Yes, yes, I can remember Sylvia saying that the school came into her calculations. Well, it doesn't. Has Tiffany spoken to Gwen about those de Morgan pots yet, by the way? I know she's never at home but it's time to be businesslike. She should do something about the desk too. It is rude not to, as well as foolish."

"It's so odd that Gwen herself hasn't said anything."

"Why odd? The executors have advised Tiffany about her legacy. It's Tiffany who's done nothing, not Gwen. By the bye, I've warned Ogier that if it's to be auction time at the castle our worthy capstan table should be included. It's shown on the inventory as part of the contents."

"Did he agree?"

"Ogier seldom says quite what is expected of him, does he? But he generally takes the point. I may tell you he is not in my best books at present. I heard via Haggarts that he's re-employing that man Hogarth. The school can employ whom they want, but I'd have expected him to have the courtesy to consult his Chairman. There isn't provision in the budget for an additional member of staff. Ogier will find I am not prepared to be a soft touch, like Drummond."

Iona decided to let it pass. "And Gwen?" she asked. "You've spoken to Gwen, I presume?"

"Gwen needs money. Look, Iona, cast your mind back to when Alex died, leaving you a widow. You felt desperately insecure. Gwen is no different. Yes, she has been left very comfortably off by our brother. But it did not exactly help, gifting the de Morgan collection to Tiffany without telling Gwen about it. You owe it to Gwen to be as objective as you can over the whole estate. And it would be wise to get the auction arranged now, while we still have the power as executors."

"How could Gwen have had Fogo put down? Fogo would have kept her company. She seemed so attached to him."

Lionel gave her a quirky smile. "She seemed so attached to Drummond. Now you'd imagine she only blames him for leaving her."

"Oh, don't say that!" Iona recoiled in dismay. After a pause she said, "Tiffany thinks I should get a little dog. What do you think, Lionel? Perhaps I could rescue an older dog from the Dog's Home. Something which was going to be put down. If I live another five years, that would be five year's remission for one little dog."

"It wouldn't be sensible to get a dog. You know what a tie they are. You need to get away. Go and spend a week with Tiffany in London. Meet some of her friends." Lionel paused, conscious that his sister was not listening. "About the auction, I'll call on Gwen as soon as I can." He went across to the dresser and examined Iona's collection of family photographs, turning as Tiffany came into the room. "My dear young niece. I gather you still have not said what you want to do about your legacy. Suppose one of those valuable bowls got broken? Or if Gwen decided to slip one into a bottom drawer?"

"Really, Lionel!" Iona exclaimed.

"If your feelings are too exquisite, I'll collect them on your behalf myself. They must be valued and insured without delay. And what about the desk?"

"I wouldn't want you to be bothered with my affairs, Uncle Lionel. Haggarts can collect everything for me. I don't know about the desk. Perhaps it could be kept here until I have a place of my own."

"But where on earth would it go?" said Iona.

"It could go in my bedroom."

"It's too big for the stairs!"

Tiffany frowned slightly. "Perhaps Gwen would like to keep it at the Dower House. The room will look very different without it."

Iona said, "You certainly shouldn't do that! Look, it could go in this room, against the far wall."

Lionel joined his hands together and flexed them. "Very well, then. That's settled. Now Tiffany, I am more than happy to speak to Gwen if you wish. I can usually influence her to advantage." He laughed uneasily, eyebrow angled. "In return, promise me to be realistic about Penwhapple. When you and Ricky were children you were going to get married and live there. Your Mother and I have just been saying what a responsibility the place is. We'll keep it in the family if we can. But not with all the clutter it has accumulated." He smiled briskly at his niece. "Is it in order to hanker for a dram? If your mother consents to raid her, quote, medicine cupboard?"

"You know I don't approve of alcohol, so I can't offer it." Iona stroked her smoothly skirted knees. "You make me wonder if I shouldn't give up the Lodge, now Sylvia is gone? With Tiffany in London I'm not sure I want to stay here anyway." Annie had been saying that Sylvia's ghost had appeared in Penwhapple . She tidied the disturbing thought aside.

"You can't possibly leave here, Mum," Tiffany declared. "What on earth would you do?"

"I really don't know. The lower half of the Dower House is about to become vacant, which seems like a sign. But I don't think I could live in such a large place after this."

Lionel said, "Think about it in the context of what happens to Penwhapple. And there's the vexed question of Somersby." Iona shifted uncomfortably. Tiffany, who until then had appeared abstracted, became still with concentration. "I have no relish for Victorian melodrama," Lionel went on. "But the situation demands that Somersby goes on the market too." He cracked his knuckles in a way Iona hated.

"How?" she asked.

Lionel shrugged. "The school has surely run its course. Under Ogier it has maintained admirable standards. But financially he's struggling. The ethos of Somersby hardly accords with present educational ideas. It's Old Hat."

"But at least Somersby has an ethos!" Tiffany spoke emotionally in defence of her old school. "Entirely relevant now, in my opinion. Something more than just preparing people for jobs!"

Lionel flinched. "Spare me the lecture! I think my grasp of what is mainstream and what is alternative is as good as yours. Somersby was conceived in a fringe society that dulled common sense with laudanum. Now it's hash. The old order changeth, yielding place to new." He stretched out his legs.

His niece frowned. "You always dismiss Somersby as quaint. But it is modern. It's been ahead of its time."

"You have heard that Mr Hal Hogarth is to be given another chance? That is bad news for a school that is struggling to keep numbers up."

"So you want the school wound up and Ogier left high and dry?"

"High and dry." Lionel savoured the phrase.

"We couldn't force Ogier's hand," Iona reasoned. "For Sylvia's sake."

"Correct. But we must face reality. Get our act together. We would have to give the school due notice, of course. But Ogier could probably be bought out for the price of a new kilt. And some frilly underwear to go with it, who knows?"

Tiffany sprang up and marched to the drawn curtains. She broke them apart and glared into the gathering dusk. The first stars were already appearing. Soon she would be back in London, where one was barely aware of stars at all. How dared Lionel poke fun at Ogier like that. She wished he could be sued. First the Rossetti, and The National Solution. Now it was sell the whole collection and rake in the cash. "It's all slipping away," she said, looking angrily at her mother.

Slipping away. Iona shifted again, uneasily. That was what Andrew Schofield had said of Sylvia. If Lionel could only think how Sylvia must be lacerated by his observations. But Lionel had never believed in life after death. Just death. Iona had heard the sound of Sylvia's voice, calling without words. If there was a hell, it was a pale and humble place, Iona told herself firmly. Heaven was what mattered. Sylvia deservedly had her place there. But possibly heaven was still Penwhapple for Sylvia, and she was unwilling to leave.

"Consider the Somersby rent. It's derisory." Lionel ignored Tiffany's back and addressed his troubled sister. "It ought to have been reviewed years ago. But of course there is no provision for that. Another of these 'grey areas,' like the school's 'right' to use the Penwhapple Glen. Think of the trouble that could give tenants."

"I quite see it could be awkward."

"How nice to have wholehearted support."

Tiffany quietly left the room.

"Your remarks about Ogier have shocked her." Iona said this as much for herself as for Tiffany.

"I thought media people were shock-proof."

"She hasn't adjusted yet. And nor, frankly, have I. One doesn't need to be a psychologist to understand how upset she feels about Sylvia's death, coming so soon after Drummond's, and so unexpectedly."

"Sylvia had had a good innings, Iona. We must not forget that."

"There is a danger, Lionel, of letting resignation sound like indifference. You could at least refrain from running people down who are still alive. Added to which, it seems the height of folly, losing all those pictures and books and ornaments. Even if one doesn't much like some of them. They have, after all, been in Penwhapple for years and years."

"One does not 'lose' valuable possessions if one realizes their value. They translate into fuller lives for us, and headaches for someone else."

Iona huddled in her chair. Then she spoke again. "Would you mind closing the curtains?" After Lionel had obliged, she went on diffidently, "I've been having such peculiar dreams."

The room became a cheerless degree colder. "Bad luck, telling your dreams," he warned her.

Iona managed a smile. "It's disconcerting. I must tell somebody."

Lionel braced himself. "Dreams of Sylvia?"

"Yes! Have you had them?"

He coughed. "I am not sufficiently sensitive."

"I dream constantly about her. Mainly she's with me in quite a dark place. I'm not sure where. Usually the castle. But she can appear when I'm in the garden. In one dream we were in her bedroom. She was in the sewing chair, muttering in the way she does sometimes, as if she was an angry mole. I couldn't believe how alive she seemed. When I woke up, I couldn't believe she was dead."

"I shouldn't let it worry you."

"Oh, I don't. She does the worrying for me. It's as if she's trying to warn us. I'm aware of her presence while I'm awake, you realise, not just at night."

"It's natural to dream about someone who was so close and has died. The rest is your imagination. Speak to Andrew Schofield."

"What could he do? I sleep very heavily, actually. I don't need any pills. But Sylvia keeps coming."

"Warning us not to sell anything else from Penwhapple? Iona, that is your guilt feelings coming out. Happens to us all, and I'm not being flippant. Take a sleeping pill tonight."

"You don't understand." Iona had begun to feel aggrieved. "You think I'm your silly little sister. But other people have had experiences. Annie and Pat have both seen Sylvia."

Lionel looked alarmed. "Hell's bells! If the McPhees spread the tidings that Sylvia's still around we'll never get the place off our hands. What nonsense have they talked?"

"Annie saw her on the tower. She was leaning over the parapet."

"Typical. Trust Annie. The tower, so original."

"Lionel." Iona began to stand up, then changed her mind. It was Sylvia who was insulted, not the McPhees. "Pat told me he distinctly felt Sylvia passing him on the first landing. And they've heard footsteps in the dining room again. I assure you, there's something peculiar going on in that house."

"Baloney. By all means keep Sylvia's memory alive. As for letting her dictate our decisions about the castle, that way lies madness. She had her say while she could. The rest is up to us. I beg you not to mention that you've seen her to anyone. And don't let the McPhees trumpet their version around either." Silence. Then, more tentatively, "Does Tiffany know?"

Iona hesitated. "She knows I feel Sylvia's presence very strongly. Tell me, Lionel, who did remove the double portrait in the end?"

Lionel's heart changed shape, then reassembled as before. "Oh God, must we go through this again? The curator person did the tricky bit. I think we lifted it down together. Why?"

"I will get the brandy after all. We could both do with just a little." Iona was gone for such a long time that Lionel could easily have had another look through the papers on her desk. She let him measure out the brandy. He gave them reasonably modest ones, passing Iona's with a steady hand. No doubt he would be unpopular if he laughed.

"Whether you or anyone else took down the portrait, the impulse to sell was yours." Fortifying herself with a sip from her glass, Iona stared anxiously at her brother.

"So I'm the next to go." Why hadn't he got Ogier to handle the thing? Detached, selfless Ogier. He considered leaving without further ado. "Iona, you're being absurd. Go and see Andrew Schofield. This talk is hysterical."

"I have never been hysterical." Iona was on her dignity again. "These dreams are not because I am ill. They are entirely real, with a purpose behind them. Possibly there's been some terrible mistake and Sylvia's trying to tell us. I know you like to mock, as Tiffany says. But we mock dreams of this sort at our peril."

More platitudinous sentimentality. Lionel bent over and kissed her robustly on the forehead. "Dear old thing, cheer up. I took down the picture, I admit it. So what?" He placed his glass on Sylvia's charming Welsh dresser. Everything was so well-ordered in the Lodge. An enlarged snapshot smiled at him, Sylvia between Tiffany and Ricky, standing beside the heron gate. There were several other framed photographs. He prepared to go. "Sylvia may haunt your dreams, but no McPhee hauntings to get about, please. If you respect your sanity and mine, keep Penwhapple environmentally friendly."

As Iona was locking the front door, Tiffany sped downstairs, her arms full of clothes. Iona followed her into the kitchen. Tiffany began stuffing garments into the washing machine with abrupt gestures. "It has to be said. Lionel is vile. We sold the Rossetti to save the castle. Now listen to him. He's a horrible uncle."

"He's the only one you've got now."

Tiffany slammed the machine shut. "I won't say he's the wrong one."

"Please don't. Lionel has your interests at heart, both with your legacy from Drummond and in discouraging unrealistic notions about Penwhapple. Do you really suppose we have not been through all this again and again? You should be grateful to Lionel."

"Mother. He wants as much money as he can squeeze out of the place. He's determined to make you move, that's obvious. He can't wait to wreck Ogier's life. So much for us, and Aunt Sylvia."

"He knows in his heart that Sylvia was Penwhapple, just as she was Somersby. It's his way of showing how upset he feels. Sylvia's gone. It's all past now. Our childhood. Drummond's wise influence, Sylvia's intense commitment. Our use for the houses."

"Blast," said Tiffany. "I've loaded my jeans without turning them inside out."

Without turning them inside out. The words repeated themselves in Iona's head. "I never mind your using the machine," she remarked. “But not so late, dear. Will you remember to switch off? And the taps?”

“You know I will.” Tiffany left the room.

Iona gave a mental shrug and told herself to check the taps. She commanded no respect. She knew nothing. Childhood. An overpowering sense of touch, or mood, or light. Alone in her sitting room, Iona longed to recapture the hours she, Sylvia and their brothers had spent together as children. To be protected again, small and vital, with no cares! A scent of apples, a subtle breeze, and she was embarking for the Fortunate Isle.

If only Sylvia had not died, she told herself unavailingly. They could talk and put their ideas straight. Beyond those modest lists of food and of sums owed, they seldom differed. If Sylvia could just reassemble then and there, they would at once understand each other. Iona felt angry with Sylvia, not for forsaking them, but for returning so ineffectively. She switched off the lights and went upstairs. Check the taps. It seemed hardly worth it. She called goodnight to Tiffany. No reply. She could not wait for Tiffany to get on with her life in London. Yet, when Tiffany was away, she missed her terribly. Perhaps she would rescue a little dog. Alex had been fond of dogs. It seemed an age since she had had a husband to discuss matters with. Dear Alex. Tiffany had been most unlucky, not to know her father.

Drummond organising a game of field cricket.

Sylvia having a good innings.

Lionel the demon bowler. “You look so nice in white, “ their Mother had said. And Lionel’s reply: “Don’t make personal remarks.” Soon afterwards he had been disparaging Iona’s feebleness with the bat, her incompetent fielding, her middle parting.

Life recapitulated. Something always elusive. It had been so much more satisfactory to be in Drummond’s team than Lionel’s. Alex, kind and considerate. Iona was certain there was life in Sylvia’s death, whatever Lionel said.

What Lionel failed to see was the possibility of death in the living.

Iona, the practical sister, sank onto her knees by the bed and prayed for Lionel’s safety. Pierced with a sense of the evil which was part of life, she began to perceive that, after all, there might indeed be a hell.

Next day Tiffany called on Lionel at Moffat and Moffats. Since she would shortly have the family's major reversionary interest in Somersby, she expected to be made a Trustee. Lionel assured her he could see no insuperable obstacle to this. Tiffany did more. She went round to George Haggart. She dealt with the matter of her legacy. She also asked him, as Secretary of the Somersby Trust, to ensure that her membership was inscribed on the agenda of the next meeting. She followed up her visit by writing to George from London. When the rescheduled summer meeting took place, Tiffany's appointment was duly made. Because of the way events moved, however, she was never to attend a meeting of the Board.

Soon after her return to London Tiffany received a letter from Haggarts confirming that her desk and the de Morgan pieces had been delivered to the Lodge. The latter were carefully unpacked by Iona, who reported at once that Bryony's Sangrail was missing. Tiffany forbad her mother to interfere. She refused to feel guilty about her Uncle Drummond. If Gwen wanted the Sangrail she could have it.

At about this time Stewart Urquhart was instructed to auction the contents of Penwhapple. An autumn date was fixed for the sale.

Chapter 19

A week before the auction, Lionel called on Gwen. His eagerness to see her gave way to disappointment when it transpired that the Schofields had got to the Dower House before him.

"How are you, Lionel?" asked Andrew Schofield, from the depth of the most comfortable chair in the room. "Bearing up?"

"Dangerous question, Andrew. I might give you a detailed answer." Lionel sat on the sofa next to Poppy. He could have taken the wing chair, but that had always been Fogo's, and smelt of dog. Not an attractive woman, Poppy, but good legs. She seemed to have lost weight. Andrew certainly had. Well, he'd managed to let two members of the Moffat family die before their time. "Don't let me disturb things." Lionel's voice suggested that any inconvenience was entirely his own. Drummond had always sat in the chair which Andrew now occupied with such limited sensibility. "The business I have with Gwen won't take long."

"Oh goodie," said Gwen. "Business." She balanced on the arm of the sofa, leaning forward to give Lionel a measure of whisky. Poppy and Andrew exchanged looks. Gwen raised her glass. "Come on, everyone. To next week's sale! I take it that's what you want to talk about, Lionel?"

"It can wait. I hope you'll be there, Poppy, plunging recklessly? I'm relying on our friends to force the prices up."

Gwen smiled. "I'm afraid there's something rather obvious about the Moffats, Poppy. If you ask me, we'll be lucky if anything sells at all. No need to give me that masterful look, Lionel." In the alcove a French mantle clock now stood, removed from Penwhapple as part of a final family share-out. Below it, on the second shelf, was a photograph of Gwen herself.

"Place isn't the same without Drummond's collection of vases," Lionel mused. "Bet you miss them, don't you?" He discerned a slight tremor in Gwen's poise. "Still, you must have felt they were a liability."

"Oh, I was never acquisitive about them. But it makes me sad when I think of the associations they had for Drummond."

Lionel treated Gwen to the raised eyebrow. "This, by the bye, is an excellent whisky."

"Come on, old thing." Andrew rose to his feet, nodding toward his wife. "Must be off."

Gwen remained seated. "Do let's hear Lionel's view before you go. Lionel always has a view. We were talking, Lionel, about the sale. What if you buy something and it turns out to have malevolent associations? I'm not superstitious, but one way and another I begin to wonder."

Lionel regarded her with a moral stare, his pale yellowish eyes bright. She had a very pretty neck. He said, "I always believe in the salutary influence of Christian prayer."

Gwen laughed. "Personally," she said, "I don't think the removal of all that clutter can come a day too soon. I remember what Drummond used to say, he who had views every bit as strong as yours, Lionel. We should none of us sacrifice ourselves for the sake of the castle."

"We must wait and see. It will be easier to find tenants once the decks are cleared. All this talk of malevolent associations is arrant nonsense, of course. Attracts the sightseers and deters serious interest."

When the Schofields had left, Lionel's manner became even more acerbic. "Thank goodness those two have gone. Not that you allowed them to cramp your style. A word in your ear about the sale. I hope you'll be attending? I'll need your support."

"Yes, Lionel?"

"Well, yes! And of course your presence would add distinction to the occasion. Encourage the collective greed."

Gwen gave him a gracious smile. "I see."

He slid his hand under her chin and, without taking his eyes from her face, kissed it. "How maddening of you to be going out this evening. Who is it you're meeting?"

"Gloria Feinstein and her friend. You see, I do everything you tell me."

"Just keep your trap shut about malevolent associations. Tell Miss Feinstein to get to the sale in good time and bring her cheque book."

" Sadly, she and her friend can't be there. Some book promotion or other. Couldn't be changed."

"Now that is seriously bad news. I had high hopes of Messrs Feinstein and Lance. Tell them to leave bids with the auctioneers."

"Oh, they'll be leaving bids. Guess who else will be at the dinner – Samantha Spencer. She should be dropping by any minute now. Here's another bit of gossip: Tiffany's friend Pippa Cursiter is having dinner with Ricky, or did you know that?"

"No, I did not know it. On the other hand, it does not altogether surprise me. I think I will make my escape before Miss Spencer arrives. You're looking so well, Gwen, and you have such amusing friends. I'm glad everyone except Lionel is having fun."

On viewing day and the day of the sale autumn rain fell ceaselessly. The stone walls of the castle were darkened. The marquee, swelling like a tumour from its side, bore up under the weight of water with dull resonance. Inside the banqueting hall furniture and effects were ranged and docketed according to the rites of sale. Penwhapple and its contents were still connected, but hanging like pearls on a defective thread.

During the lunch interval Lionel presided over a table in the marquee. He was attentive, but not too attentive, to the widowed sister-in-law by his side. Gwen's presence he now saw as ill-omened. The sale had got off to an inauspicious start, with lot after lot selling below estimate.

"We've been unlucky with the weather," said Stewart Urquhart, dropping his voice. "It's usually so reliable at this time of year. And, you know, it is unfortunate that so many items were withdrawn after the catalogue had been agreed. Gives an impression the sale lacks quality. Nonsense of course. Plenty of scholarly interest. Perhaps not quite enough – don't know how to put this – designer appeal. They liked that Aesthetic Movement chair. The tapestries went well too."

"Where are the London dealers, the hot-heads? We seem to have attracted the local Civic Society and a few retired civil servants. The sale looks set to be a disaster."

"I have some hopes for the afternoon session, especially the paintings. Swings and roundabouts. I say. Look who's arrived." Ogier had entered the tent.

He approached the table at which the eleventh laird and his cronies were feasting. Lionel's spirits lifted. He forgave Ogier his shabby kilt and eccentric appearance, recognizing him fleetingly as his peer. Lionel stood. With a wave of his hand he commanded silence. "Quiet, please, everyone. This is important. The Headmaster of Somersby!" Poised behind the high table, he leant forward, smiling in the face of Ogier's unfaltering advance.

Ogier acknowledged Lionel's challenge good humouredly. "I came to congratulate Urquharts on their catalogue. A thorough and scholarly job." Up to this point the silence commanded by Lionel had extended no further than those gathered round him. Now an uneasy quiet fell more widely. Neither Ogier or Lionel appeared perturbed. Ogier continued, "I was surprised to see some of the lots which have been included. There are items of panelling, for example, which surely ought to be treated as part of the fabric." He and Lionel stared balefully at each other. No more was said.

"I had better get back to the sale room," said Stewart Urquhart.

Lionel sat down. Ogier bought himself a cup of coffee. General conversation resumed. Conscious that a damaging blow had been struck, Lionel was nevertheless undaunted. If the Puritans wanted a fight they would need a more potent champion than Ogier.

Ogier and Lionel made their way to the banqueting hall, its noble scale diminished by the auctioneer's stand, the rows of chairs, many of them in the sale, and the clutter of other lots, sold and unsold. Ogier moved close to lot 84, part of the morning session, a carved oak press bearing the date 1683. Lying on it were some small items, also sold, including an engraved steel trowel, SWM, 10 March 1883. With it Sholto Moffaat had laid the foundation stone of the banqueting hall.

Bidding commenced briskly, Stewart Urquhart bringing down the gavel again and again. A pair of Moffat tocher chairs reached £1,200, a price with which the local museum seemed well satisfied. There followed the pair of carved oak armchairs in which Byrony and Sholto had sat on either side of the fireplace. £2,800. Good interior designer items. Now came the Penwhapple state bed, only the footboard and embroidered canopy on show, the bear and pipe-playing monkey mocking the assembled company. £2,200.

"Someone got a bargain there," said a voice at Ogier's side. It was Hal Hogarth, his eyes fixed on the auctioneer.

Christina Rossetti's half tester bed followed. At £900 it was the first lot that afternoon to exceed Urquhart's estimate.

That cleared the furniture. Now Urquharts proceeded to dispose of Sholto and his sister as artists, beginning with a pencil and watercolour view: Penwhapple Castle with Ailsa Craig in the distance, c1870. At £420, it was up to estimate. Lot 138, Bryony Moffat's The Bridal of Triermain, oil, signed with monogram, was sold well below. Next, Our Grandmother, another of Bryony's watercolours, her Boyd grandmother decked in an eighteenth-century gown, with her lap dogs. A watercolour by Sholto, The Haunted House, All-Hallow's Eve. A group of pencil studies made by Sholto in the Penwhapple Glen.

> "As we sat painting together by the rushing
> Penwhapple stream there had never occurred a
> misunderstood word or wish which might divide us."

The brutal gavel knocked the drawings down for £240. So far all the pictures except the first had been sold below estimate.

A monochrome by Arthur Hughes was held aloft, another well-loved picture: Bryony and Sholto seated in the banqueting hall, she at the table, he in his oak chair, Fogo at Bryony's feet. An atmosphere of perfect peace. Ogier resisted the temptation to put up his hand. All too soon the picture was removed.

Arthur Hughes's The Staircase at Penwhapple. This went to the local museum for £1,400, a good price, up to estimate. Now another painting by Bryony Moffat, an oil this time, The Ruined Church at Penwhapple, with grazing sheep and Ailsa Craig in the distance. Next, Old Dailly Churchyard. Lionel went to stand near the rostrum, his manner inscrutable, mouth slightly smiling.

Bryony Moffat seated on her stool, painting the studio from which Sholto was emerging, book in hand, apple blossom over Bryony's head. An idyll of harmony, friendship, animals, endless talk. A few locals had been buying, but piece by piece, concentrating on the modest items. The dealers had little competition for the more expensive pictures, many of which sold poorly. The representative of the local museum seemed to have an understanding with his colleague from Edinburgh. Bell Scott's portrait of Sholto Moffat,

Eighth Laird, full length, in shooting jacket with his double-barrelled hammer twelve bore, went for £1,100.

"Lot number 150."

"Here, sir!"

Sholto Moffat's Study of Fogo, his sister's dog, signed with monogram, inscribed Cave Canem. Brown wash, heightened with white. The bidding began at twenty pounds.

Ogier felt a simmering of fierce intent. He addressed himself to that farouche portrait as though committed by an assurance given to Sylvia herself. A private bidder and the representative of the local museum were erecting an abstract ladder, rung by five-pound rung. The private buyer dropped out. A woman to Ogier's left came in. The rungs began to go up ten pounds at a time, then twenty. £320. £340. £360. £380. Silence fell.

"Three hundred and ninety, then. I'll take three hundred and ninety."

The woman indicated assent. Silence fell for a second time. As the gavel was about to fall, Ogier fluttered his catalogue.

"Four hundred? Thank you, sir, four hundred. Four hundred and twenty. Four hundred and forty. Four hundred and sixty. Five hundred?" Inwardly, Ogier faltered. He had not expected such a large increase. He had meant to drop out before five hundred. Again he was aware of Hal Hogarth beside him. He fluttered his catalogue. "At five hundred pounds. Yours, sir, for five hundred pounds." From the corner of his eye, Ogier saw Lionel in motion.

"Five hundred and fifty. Five hundred and fifty." Stewart Urquhart looked at Ogier with no friendly eye. Hal Hogarth shifted his stance in a gesture of solidarity. "Six hundred. Six hundred and fifty. Seven hundred. Thank you, sir. Yours for seven hundred pounds." Fogo stared humorously askance, eyes blank yet all-seeing. At seven hundred, Lionel stalled. Nothing would induce him to go higher and risk being landed with that brute, with its evil bat's wing feet. His eye met Ogier's in a clinch. He nodded to Stewart Urquhart. "Seven hundred and fifty." The auctioneer looked at Ogier. "Against you, sir." Ogier waited until the gavel was about to descend, then fluttered his catalogue again.

"Eight hundred. At eight hundred pounds." Lionel saw Gwen watching him. So Ogier was making the running. Let him exert himself then. Let him drain his meager resources. Coolly enough,

Lionel calculated whether he could possibly squeeze another bid out of his cousin. Across his mind flashed the image of Drummond's unruly dog, eyes glittering, watching his master in this very room. Catching his eye, Stewart Urquhart said, "Ten if you like." Lionel nodded.

"At eight hundred and ten. Against you, sir. Eight hundred and twenty. Eight hundred and thirty. Eight hundred and forty."

A long pause, and the gavel came down at last. Ogier had acquired the only picture in the sale to double its estimate.

When the sale was over, Gwen made her way to Lionel's side. "Bother Ogier," she said. "I wanted you to have that picture. I could see from Ogier's face he was determined to get it."

Lionel vowed in silence that Ogier would not be allowed to gloat. The sale had been a disaster. He had not kept a running tally, but the total was well below Stewart Urquhart's "worst case scenario." He controlled his anger by maintaining a courteous façade toward his sister-in-law.

He had dinner with Iona, who tried to put a good face on the outcome. They had a long talk about Iona's position at the Lodge. The house was part of the family Trust, and jointly owned. They agreed the best course would be for Iona to remain there while the castle was empty. In that way she could keep an eye on the place. If the new tenants wanted the Lodge as well as the castle they could have it. If not, Iona could reconsider her position. She could wait and see what the new neighbours were like. The possibility of rerouting the drive could be explored, to give her more privacy. Iona said she was inclined to think that if the drive were rerouted she might end up with less privacy than under the existing arrangement. There was no need to contemplate unnecessary expense. There was something uncannily sane about the way she talked through this painful subject.

Driving away, Lionel had an idea. It was time to arrange a fuller, more businesslike talk with Gwen. He could go round now, it was not too late. Sternly, he took himself in hand. He would wait a day or two. And he would not just drop round unannounced. He would arrange something enjoyable for Gwen. He might suggest an outing for her and Iona, dinner perhaps.

Feeling virtuous, Lionel went home.

It was not until a few days later, when he went through the report in detail, that he discovered how well the Canadians had done at the Penwhapple sale. They had adopted a policy of leaving conservative bids on lots which interested them. On one or two important items, such as the state bed, they had been underbidders.

Lionel determined to recoup what he saw as his losses when it came to negotiating the Penwhapple lease. That, he told himself, was the next step.

Chapter 20

Ogier had intended to present the picture of Fogo to the school immediately after the Penwhapple sale. Three weeks passed, and he had done nothing. The picture remained in its makeshift cardboard wrapping, propped against the filing cabinet.

It was a Thursday morning, the time Ogier reserved for dealing with correspondence. In the past he had sometimes dropped in to talk with Pippa, a practice he had now stopped. Today he needed to see her again. Looking at the unopened parcel, it occurred to him that he could deploy the dog as an impromptu ambassador. He went to the window and gazed for a while at the view which had so often given him inspiration.

The gently sloping lawn in front of the Mansion was normally out of bounds, but a special dispensation had been given to the hockey team. They were there now, practising a sweeping manoeuvre. Beyond the lawn were the sentinel trees, a pair of well grown beeches, and a smaller copper beech beside the hand gate to the park. In the spring it was the copper beech which gave the view its enchantment. In the autumn it was the turn of the massive, many-branched common beeches. Having turned first to yellow, and then to orange, the old trees were now a brilliant red. A ball went wide. Shouts came up from the hockey players. They tried again. Ogier wished he had bought something personal for Pippa at the Penwhapple sale.

A bell sounded. The hockey practice broke up. Children returned to their classrooms. Ogier decided to wait exactly twelve minutes and then set off. At the college meeting Pippa had sat across from him, at a shallow angle. He recalled her expression, mouth ready to smile, eyes watchfully serious. At exactly the time selected he opened the door of her classroom. She was wearing a peach coloured scarf. “Oh, hello,” she said briefly, glancing back at her papers.

He sauntered in, closing the door, aware of her active pen, her bent head. "May I interrupt a moment?"

"Of course." The pen halted.

Ogier perched across a desk. He felt her intensity as something noble. He wanted to speak first, have the advantage, work round to the real purpose of his visit. He launched forth, surprising even himself. "I wonder if we might speak informally about what is going on behind my back - if I can put it that way without sounding too paranoid." He regarded the classroom clock as if to reassure her. "Can you tell me what lay behind the argument at yesterday's College meeting?"

Pippa laid the pen down. She tilted up her chin. "You let us have our brainstorming session. A free-for-all of ideas. It went perfectly, thanks to you."

"Let me be candid, Pippa. The Dower House. Could you tell me anything about that?"

"You shouldn't take rumours too seriously." Pippa smiled disarmingly. She fiddled with her pen. "The discussion went well. I wish you would leave it at that."

Ogier smiled too. "Something everyone seems to know about can hardly be called a rumour."

Pippa bent her tawny head and the light through the window burnished every hair. At last she said earnestly, "At the moment we are catering for middle class parents with two cars, Ogier. We ought to be available for the less fortunate in society. That means working in an urban environment. It's quite reasonable of Sam. I agree it's difficult putting theory into practice. Moving away lock, stock and barrel."

"I have something I want to show you," said Ogier. He laid the parcel containing Sholto's study of Fogo on Pippa's desk and began to undo it. "This is what I bought at the Penwhapple sale. Your friendship has meant a great deal to me, Pippa." He shifted his perch on the desk.

A shaft of sunlight fell across the picture. Pippa's delight was not so much in Sholto's old mongrel as in the romance attached to Ogier's gesture. So this was the picture for which had paid almost a thousand pounds. The details of the transaction were so well known in the staff room as to constitute a minor scandal. She would have the picture in her bed sitting room. It would look amusing over the bed. She would write and tell Tiffany.

There was a short silence. Her peach scarf, the skirt of some grey stuff falling in soft folds. Ogier longed to move close to her, pull her gently against him. "This was a picture Sylvia particularly liked," he said. "She felt it gave children confidence in the animal kingdom."

Pippa turned her face towards him with the serene expression which so pleased him. "Ogier dear, I will treasure the picture, for your sake and of course for Sylvia's too." She looked down, then raised her eyes to meet his, wondering why he had not given Fogo's portrait to Tiffany. Well, he hadn't. He had given it to her.

Neither of them spoke. Then Ogier said, "It's terrible loving you when you can't love me." Her lips parted as she prepared to answer him. Deliberately he went on, "Please put up this picture in the classroom where it can in a sense belong to us all."

Pippa's smile faded. "Very well," she said, softly. Rallying a more impersonal tone she went on, "Don't let the past dictate your decisions about Somersby, Ogier. It could lead you astray."

"You lead me astray," he murmured. His changing expression kept pace with his thoughts. "You enhance everything. Physically, intellectually and emotionally."

"Ogier, you are the superior being. Too lofty to share yourself with a woman." She grasped his hand and, in a gesture of dramatic renunciation, dropped it and moved to the window. They could hear the sound of young children dragging a go-cart, their voices straying innocently into the room. The youngsters chased off with cheerful yells. Pippa said, without looking at him, "I've loved Somersby. I've loved you, but not in the way you want me to love you, and which I know would make you unhappy. Tiffany always says you are Somersby, the legend and the future. You must see me as a more ordinary mortal."

The door opened and Samantha walked in. "Ah, you're both here. Good. I wanted you in particular, Pippa." She looked breezily from one to the other. "It's rather urgent."

Pippa lounged against one of the desks, smiling, and extending her fingers across the wooden top. "We'll go to the art room, shall we? I've a short while before taking a lesson there. Would that suit?" Her glance included Ogier. As she passed him, she picked up the picture of Fogo.

Samantha pretended not to see it, and was filled with a wave of anger. "Sometime, Ogier, I'd like a session with you too, if you could let me know when. There's just one thing now. I'll follow you, Pippa." She waited until Pippa had gone. "She seems to assume she can do exactly what she wants. There's always trouble in the playground with her class. They're reasonable with her but little demons with everyone else. If you won't speak to her, I will."

"I have spoken to her. As you can see."

"It's not just the playground. I've been trying to get her class started on their French. They are impossible. It's one of the things she and I need to discuss. Perhaps you should take a hand at teaching them sometime. Then you'd know."

"Samantha, I don't think we need a session together. We will be finalising the accounts with the Trustees next week. I ask you to remember what Lionel said: the policy is in the figures."

Samantha left the room, somewhat disconcerted. She recalled the portrait of Fogo in Pippa's hands. I must challenge Ogier for the chairmanship of the College of Teachers, she decided. In Bryony's day the chairmanship had changed every year as a matter of routine. Two years had been the longest any one teacher had held the position. It was an abuse, Ogier's holding it so long.

That evening Pippa hung the picture of Fogo above her bed and dashed off a note to Tiffany. She started with news of Ricky. He had been made a partner in Moffat and Moffats. To mark the occasion, Lionel had thrown a big party, "which needless to say I had a great time at, while behaving myself. Ogier has been rather odd lately. School politics getting him down. The picture I told you about, the one Ogier bought, well - hold your breath - it's here in the cottage! He gave it to me! What a sweet man. He was most supportive about that row I got into, by the way. More of that when I see you. I feel sorry for children nowadays. At least Somersby doesn't take their childhood away. It's definitely the education I want for my children – supposing I have any! Sorry, no time for more. Must prepare tomorrow's lesson. Big row with Samantha over French. The class can't stand it, especially the boys!"

Chapter 21

"What the blazes are you doing?" Lionel expostulated. "Martyring yourself to this place!"

Iona eased her back. She held the dustpan at a distance, glancing round with flustered resignation. "Someone must keep it looking decent." They were in the library at Penwhapple, a room which no longer had its panelling or its wall decorations or even its curtain rods. "You know Annie won't come near Penwhapple unless I'm here too. I have to show a presence."

Lionel threw open one of the windows. Gwen gave him an anxious glance. A draught of bitter air prowled across the room. Iona went to the window, shook a duster outside and fastened it shut again.

"Even the postman won't come up here. He leaves the mail with me now."

"Well of course he does. You asked him to, remember? My dear sister, I can't believe there are no sane people in this area."

"I can't rely on the McPhees." Iona spoke testily. "They've plenty to do at the school." She surveyed the forlorn room, as if it were furnished, polished and decorated for a glittering social function. "That's all right. I think I've finished in here." She went to the door, invited them to pass through, shut it, locked it and then stood still for a moment, listening. "I'll just do the summer parlour then."

Lionel and Gwen followed her up the dismally cold stairs, unease running between them. "No heavy stuff, mind," Lionel told her. "A glance only, to make sure the jackdaws have not got in." Their feet echoed across bare boards. The summer parlour was even more depressing than the library. The batons which had secured the tapestries remained, splintered where Sholto's craftsmanship had frustrated the removal men. And then, the gothic lettering above the chimney piece:

Move. Not. This. Picture. Let. It. Be.
For. Love. Of. Those. In. Effigy.

"All correct," Lionel pronounced, squaring his tweed shoulders. "Come on, let's get back to civilisation. We don't need a tour, thank you." Iona had shrunk, he thought, the way Sylvia had. A shrunken frame, and suddenly frail. Not the stalwart Iona of a year ago.

"I saw Sylvia again yesterday," she said in an off-hand voice.

"Whatever do you mean?" Gwen gasped.

"She means Sylvia's personality is very much in evidence," Lionel supplied. "She's still around. I can feel her too. It's rather comforting."

"Don't be sentimental Lionel." Iona moved across the landing. "It doesn't suit you. Call a spade a spade, as you usually do. I saw Sylvia herself."

"Now listen to me," her brother said sternly, halting their progress. "You really mustn't talk like that. We all feel Sylvia. We all know there's something tangible living on here. Of course we do."

"Of course. It's perfectly natural," Gwen confirmed, touching Iona's wrist.

Iona made a gesture of impatience. "She was in her bedroom. It wasn't specially natural because she didn't speak. But I understood what passed between us."

"Ah. Well. You were always very close," Lionel was able to say. "But it is no good building up stories which cannot possibly be verified and which make the castle sound evil. We will never find tenants that way."

"Lionel's quite right you know, Iona. Those two Canadian ladies have drawn right back, and they were so promising. I don't think they're nervous about the paranormal themselves. But they're concerned about getting cleaning help and so on."

They stepped downstairs, their feet ringing round them. Iona broke off to inspect the kitchen. The deal cupboards had gone. A dead bluebottle lay on the windowsill. Iona walked over and gave it her full attention. "That wasn't here yesterday," she announced.

"We aren't hygiene inspectors," Lionel chaffed. "Come along, dear."

Iona closed the door, locked it and then stood listening expectantly. They descended to the hall. "What was that?" she demanded, swinging round. Again she stood in an expectant attitude, looking aslant into Lionel's face. He took her by the elbow and manoeuvred her through the inner door, then, even more firmly, through the heavy outer door. It's massive bulk came between them and the sombre spaces within with a satisfactory thump.

"I'll make sure Pat and Annie come at least twice a week," Lionel told his sister. "Holding hands, if needs be. We must get the central heating working properly. In fact, I intend to have some internal repairs done. All that battening looks depressing. We'll do what Urquharts suggested and use some old window shuttering where those panels used to be. I don't know what we do about the summer parlour. Some furnishing material to replace the tapestries, perhaps. It needn't be expensive. I'll get Ricky to see to it. You don't have to set foot in here again. It's not doing you any good, pottering about with a duster and feeling miserable. We have contract cleaners to feel miserable for us. As for showing a presence, as you call it, that's the job of the McPhees."

"Not miserable," Iona answered lightly. "Not really. Nothing has changed, for me. Nothing essential, that is. I miss Tiffany, of course."

They went down the drive. "I do wish you had come to the party Lionel gave for Ricky," Gwen said, tucking her arm through Iona's.

"Yes," said Lionel. "He was upset not to see you. He made quite an amusing little speech. Said some nice things about the staff. I was suprised he could be so tactful."

"He spoke so affectionately about everyone. I felt better after such a happy family occasion. Drummond always had great faith in Ricky."

"He had to get a crack in at me of course. Assured everyone that so long as I was there nothing would change. Well, he's a partner now. How soon before he expects a new car."

They walked three abreast up the Lodge path. After a muddle with her key, Iona opened the door, saying, "I wonder when Ricky will settle down." A little black dog came bounding out. This was Tottie, rescued by Iona from the dogs' home against all advice. First she jumped up at Gwen. Then she jumped up at Lionel. Then she ran into the middle of Iona's small lawn and squatted. "The gate!" exclaimed Iona. "Did we shut the gate?" She hurried quickly down the path, checked the gate and returned. The dog was jumping up at Gwen again, dodging out of reach when Iona tried to intervene.

"What about that coffee?" Lionel asked. "The castle wasn't exactly on our agenda, you know." He contrived to seem open and confiding.

Iona stood holding the door, blocking their way. "I hope she hasn't laddered your tights, Gwen?"

"Coffee, Iona? It's not two yet," Lionel pointed out. "Does coffee feature in your life these days?"

She turned her deep set eyes upon him, very guilelessly regarding him under her fringe. "Forgive me if I don't ask you in. I feel awfully tired suddenly. I'll just sit quietly for a bit."

"Very well," said Lionel. "You have a rest. Don't let that wretched dog interfere."

Gwen kissed Iona affectionately. "Take care now," she said.

At the gate Lionel looked at Iona with considerable misgivings. "We'll go back via Somersby and have a word with Pat and Annie." He paused. "No going to the castle yourself, remember. You've promised! Now, dog, you stay in the garden and guard the house."

Iona waved them away. She checked the gate, satisfying herself that Lionel and Gwen had really gone. Lionel was too managerial. He would put a stop to everything if he could.

Iona had become very secretive. She settled herself in the window, where she could watch Tottie sniffing about. The next moment Antony and his Mother were at the gate. Iona went to see her visitors, observing with amusement how Antony asserted his schoolboy dignity as she approached. She refrained from embracing him, as had been Sylvia's way. It was not hers.

"You won't let him tire you?" Alison spoke from the spot where Lionel had paused. "It's so good of you to have him like this. I'll be back as soon as the double art period is over."

"Don't do that. We'll come down to Somersby together."

"Are you sure? It's not too far for you?"

"Certainly not! It's a good routine we've got. I'll bring him to the art room, shall I?"

"That would be a help. He's had his lunch."

"Perfectly all right," said Iona. "We'll amuse each other." Her eyes dwelt on the top of Antony's smooth head. He was dressed like a proper Somersby boy, in sensible clothes. She ushered him inside, leaving Alison to make her escape. "Don't forget to close the gate," she called after her.

Antony had made straight for the kitchen. "Auntie Sylvia let me do everything," he stated. Then, after a pause, "Can I have some sticky bread?"

"What about a piece of plain bread, with gooseberry jam?"

Antony smiled. "With raspberry jam!"

Iona searched her shelf. She had strawberry. The distinction need not be made. "Here you are then." She made some for Tottie as well, and fed it to her in small bits.

Antony munched. "Which do you like best," he asked, "old fashioned or modern?"

"Modern," said Iona firmly.

Antony went to the window and peered out, kneeling on a chair, "Can we go to the castle?"

Iona hesitated. "It's all empty, remember."

"Auntie Sylvia won't be there. I know."

"Well, your Aunt Sylvia is, and isn't there. She's gone to heaven, but her soul is still alive. She watches over the castle because she loved it."

"How is she still alive?"

"Try to picture her the same but - well, glassy."

"Will I see her?" Antony's face was tense.

"Certainly not."

"Let's go up," he said. They walked along the drive, Antony holding Tottie. The dog played about, trying to snatch the lead from him. As the castle came into view she became subdued. She walked closer to Iona, bumping into her legs. Sylvia will be very near now, Iona told herself. "Have you heard the bell ring?" Antony demanded.

"Not the bell. Tottie has heard Fogo barking."

"I heard him too." Antony swept his free arm. "I saw him sitting on the stairs." Iona received this information in silence. Antony pulled her hand. "Can we go to my bridge?"

Iona was wearing stout shoes. She had often warned Sylvia against negotiating that steep path, invariably slippery even in summer. "I think Tottie would get muddy. We couldn't have her in the sitting room with us. We'd have to towel her first."

Antony screwed up his face at her. "Please," he said, wistfully.

"It so happens I've got my walking shoes on. We could go just as far as the bridge. Then home." Antony struck off, cheerful to be leaving the castle behind. Iona followed at a snail's pace, cross with herself for giving in. "Don't let Tottie off the lead," she called, too late. As they stood on the bridge the sun came out.

"Please can we go just a bit further?" Antony pleaded.

The sunshine through the trees was enticing. "Just a short way then." Tottie was running down to the water's edge, then running back again. The fur on her legs was already covered in mud.

Antony took Iona's hand. "I don't believe anyone's seen Aunt Sylvia," he declared. "She's dead now. I don't want anyone to see her."

"Just remember Aunt Sylvia as she used to be. Happy in your company. That's what I do."

"But don't say you see her."

"Very well." They walked in silence. The path became narrow. She let Antony go in front. "We must be back soon. I don't want to make you late for Mummy."

"We haven't got to the pool yet."

"It's too far. I said just to the bridge." Antony set off, running. Tottie left the stream and ran with him, splattering him with mud. "Ant! We haven't time. Come here please!" He ran on, seeming not to hear her. Muttering under her breath, Iona followed. By the time she caught up, Antony was on the rock above the Rossetti pool. He leaned out as far as he could, staring into its depths. "Be careful!" Iona called sharply.

He came away. "It's full of shadowy things."

"It's full of water. And you can't swim."

Again, he seemed not to hear. "I can see something," he faltered, concentrating on the water, stooping dangerously over the edge of rock. "Look in there," he cried.

Iona searched the brackish surface. What lay beneath was a mystery. "There's nothing," she said curtly, grasping his upper arm. He wrenched away. Iona was unbalanced. When she clutched at him, he fended her off. She flung an arm randomly in the air, while the other beat her chest. She seemed struck with cramp as she plunged sideways into the pool.

Antony's mouth gaped in a stricken face. Iona was floating quietly. She started to thresh, head low in the water. She rolled forward in a gentle somersault, her pleated skirt rising toward the surface. Her hands, well below, glimmered white. The distressed water was full of bubbles. Antony bent over the brink, crying wildly, "She's down there! I know she's down there!" He watched intently, waiting for Iona to clamber out. But her clothes, sucking at what little air lay beneath them, were twirling her beyond recall. He squeezed his eyes in a violent grimace, gasped for breath and fled back along the path.

At the bridge he halted, listened, and stared at the stone tower above him. Darting over the converging streams he scrambled uphill, crying in agitation. Tottie ran with him, then stopped. She ran another short distance at his side. She went back, looking for Iona.

Crossing the castle forecourt on the way home, and covered in mud, Antony panicked, thinking he heard a rogue toll from the castle bell. As soon as he was safely past he began running in the direction of Iona's Lodge, hoping to find his mother. She was not there. He ran to the road. It was only a short distance to the entrance to Somersby. He was forbidden to go on the road unaccompanied. He went out, walking, looking about him, sure he was being followed. He turned in towards Somersby at last. At the cottages he started to run again. When he reached the art room his mother was still teaching. He assumed an air of nonchalance. He played outside until her class was over.

Alison was concerned by the state he was in. He told her he had spotted a pheasant behind the castle. Mrs Ramsay had said it was special for a pheasant to be friendly, and this one had come right up close. Alison, though still puzzled, was reassured, and got the worst of the mud off him. He gave her an excited account of how Tottie had kept jumping up at him.

Only at dusk was the alarm raised, when Hal found Tottie wandering on the drive. A police search party with special lighting went down the Penwhapple Glen. Iona's body was wedged under a gnarled root in the Rossetti Pool. At the post mortem it was recorded she had died of a heart attack.

Chapter 22

Iona was cremated. The Vicar of Holy Trinity gave the address. An anthem followed, sung by Tiffany, who came forward and stood facing the mourners. Pippa held her breath in a thrill of dismay, unaware that Tiffany had more than once suspended disbelief on her behalf. Tiffany's voice was amateurish. It bothered Pippa that Tiffany wore her hat to sing.

Tiffany had wanted to offer hospitality at Iona's house after the service. She had been persuaded this would be impracticable. Light refreshments were provided at the Dower House instead. At Tiffany's insistence the occasion was alcohol-free, in deference to Iona's memory.

"An unusual family," Poppy Schofield remarked to her husband, as they passed the alcove in which Gwen's French clock was displayed.

"Yes. Original and talented. It's very sad to have lost three members in so short a time."

"A word of advice, Andrew," drawled Lionel. "Officially we're nonalcoholic. Unofficially try slipping through to the kitchen later in the proceedings. I will give you a signal."

"A cup of tea will be fine by us. We won't be staying long. Just wanted to let you know how sorry we are. An interesting address, I thought. I had forgotten about Iona's time in the tropics. When Tiffany stood up to sing it was most moving."

Quite, thought Lionel. How long, he wondered, before the Curse of Penwhapple struck again. "Come on Andrew," he said. "Let's sneak to the kitchen now. No sense delaying matters." He looked round at Poppy, asking if he could bring her anything.

"Perhaps Andrew could find an orange juice for me. Something long. I don't feel like tea, as it happens." She made her way across to Tiffany. Gwen was nearby, about to join them.

Ricky intercepted his father as he and Andrew emerged from

the kitchen. "Successful expedition, Dad?"

"Very. We were getting Poppy an orange juice. Here's the proof." He raised the glass. "Your little friend Miss Cursiter is looking radiant, incidentally." Lionel paused, subjecting Pippa to detached scrutiny. "Radiant in Black."

"George Haggart certainly seems to think so."

"Friendly, susceptible George Haggart."

"You're well out of that girl," said Lionel to his son. "Tell me the truth. Are you fonder of her than you let on? Say if I'm intruding, and I'll shut up."

Ricky made himself treat Lionel's question as a joke. "Perhaps I was getting a bit serious. I don't know. Anyway, Dad, you needn't worry. I know your opinion of her. Can't think what I saw in her myself, actually."

"She'd henpeck you. I know the type. Not that I want to interfere."

"But that's a law of nature isn't it, as far as you're concerned? All women henpeck their husbands."

"Possibly. One day maybe you'll admit your father was not such a fool in that respect. Nevertheless there are degrees. Your little Miss Cursiter has a quite exceptional aptitude for giving men hell in my opinion. Come on, we must talk to Tiffany. She seems to be finding the occasion rather a strain."

Tiffany was deep in conversation with Ogier. She was planning to establish a Trust Fund for the benefit of Somersby. "I had thought of buying out the family interest in Penwhapple, making it available to the school again. Probably cost me less than a new flat in London. Ogier, you have a quite uncanny way of listening and saying nothing. Tell me honestly, is this the best way I can help the school? You see, if I bought Penwhapple I could return and take an interest in everything. The way Sylvia did. I could even imagine myself as a teacher one day."

"Come and see me at Somersby tomorrow." Ogier put off thinking of Tiffany as a teacher. "I may not be Chairman of the College much longer. The idea is I might hand over in the summer." Ogier was conscious of suppressing his real feelings. "You mustn't sacrifice your career for the sake of the school - that is not what Sylvia would have wanted. Your task is to carry the idealism you learnt at Somersby into your work. If it means a career in London and presenting your own TV programme, so be it. That was your aim in life, wasn't it? The BBC?"

"Yes, the World Service! I don't know where presenting my own TV programme comes in."

"There is one other matter. There's disagreement within the College about the future for Somersby. The school you think you are helping could look very different in a year or two. I'll give you a run-down tomorrow. The best way you can help is not with money, but by attending the meeting of the Trustees in February, the major policy meeting of the year."

"I don't think I can come, Ogier. The legislative timetable has been allowed to slip. I thought I'd explained that." The hint of strain reappeared. Tiffany had refused to take off her hat. She looked faintly deranged

"Come along, Tiffany, you haven't eaten a thing. I am instructed by Gwen to get you and Ogier up to the buffet." There was an edginess in Lionel's manner. "And I'm afraid you are going to have to talk to your mother's co-driver from Meals on Wheels. A government supporter. Rather an old-fashioned one, between ourselves. She dislikes developments in voluntary sector policy. You may have some explaining to do."

There was a general move towards the buffet. Iona's friend turned out not to have been a co-driver from Meals on Wheels but a representative of the British Red Cross.

When the reception was over Ogier gave Samantha a lift to Somersby. Tiffany went back with Pippa, who had parked some way from the Dower House. They had an altercation about whether Tiffany should spend the night at the Lodge, or go back with Pippa.

"Hello, you two. What's the matter? Won't this thing start?" It was Ricky, who had followed them with an agenda of his own.

"Tiffany insists on spending the night at that freezing Lodge. It's so stupid, tonight of all nights. Tell her she's to come with me. You come too, Ricky. You can treat us to a drink in Crossways."

He felt a pang of affection for Pippa. "Not in that car. Nothing would induce me."

"Of course not, come in your own monster, we're not inviting you to spend the night."

"Very well, I will follow at a respectful distance."

"Good."

During the night the rain stopped. Tiffany was not mentally prepared for the tasks waiting in her mother's little house. After breakfast she decided to take a look at the castle. At the last bend in the drive she turned aside, wandering up the lawn and into the enclosed garden. Here she quickened her steps, dodging crabbed fruit trees, skirting the conservatory by the stork gates, now without their storks. At the top of the garden, she turned.

It was not as she remembered. The Penwhapple of her imagination loomed so large that reality conjured up something only approximate. Her eyes scrutinised the pepperpot turrets and disproportionate chimney stack. From one of the chimney pots a wisp of smoke arose. They must have fixed the central heating. The banqueting hall was in shadow. At this distance the bell house was barely distinguishable. The pastry-top tower was in sunlight. Slowly Tiffany walked back through the garden, straight towards the castle, forcing herself to confront her sense of loss. Everything was unreal. Without its contents Penwhapple was a stony reproach. With great firmness Tiffany turned her mind to the problem of her mother's possessions. The side tables, the photographs - everything over which Iona took so much trouble. It had all become a burden. She spent the rest of the morning going through her mother's clothes.

It was almost lunchtime when she remembered her promise to look up Ogier. She telephoned and left a message, saying she would be in touch later. In the afternoon she lost all sense of time, leafing through old photographs. Eventually she shoved them into Drummond's desk. At dinner with Lionel she could report that Iona's possessions were in order. Gwen told her she was "so practical" - her mother's daughter.

Looking at Tiffany's strained face, Lionel concurred. But Tiffany was toying with her food. Her technique was to scrape at it, arranging a mouthful on her fork. Then she would let it fall and start again. Lionel wondered guiltily what she would do for Christmas and Hogmanay.

Chapter 23

The Somersby budget meeting took place in early February, when Samantha tabled a proposal that the school move to Ayr. The education authority, she reported, was prepared to lease a redundant property on reasonable terms. Tiffany failed to attend the meeting or comment then or later on Samantha's document.

A week afterwards Lionel received a letter from George Haggart. He summoned Ricky to discuss it at once, and was already on the telephone when Ricky entered the room. "Read that," Lionel told him tersely, flicking George's letter across the desk. He did not break off his conversation. "And who did you say was acting for them? The big Glasgow firm? Yes of course I've seen their letter. What I am concerned about is the standing of this Glasgow outfit. Are they wide boys who will try anything once? Do we treat this as a joke?" He listened impatiently to George Haggart's conscientious reply. "Look, George, Ricky has joined me. I think we'll go over to the blower. Don't get the idea you've been cut off. I'll transfer us now."

Lionel pressed a button on the handset of the new telephone. He then replaced the receiver and jiggled it. Ricky shifted uncomfortably. The jiggle was an unnecessary refinement. It seemed probable that George would be cut off after all.

"Can you hear me George?"

"Loud and clear, Lionel."

"Excellent. Ricky is with me. Come in please, Ricky. Hadn't you better sit closer to the microphone?"

"George, good morning. Can you hear me?" Ricky made no attempt to move.

"Hearing you fine, Ricky. Good morning."

"Ricky has your letter in front of him. So you see this as a serious offer for the freehold of the castle."

"I read the letter as a formal offer under Scottish law."

"Correct. But the price George. You realise this is well short of what we require for a lease, let alone the freehold."

"Quite so."

"How did the Glasgow lot explain that when you spoke to them?"

"They say their clients are offering a fair market price. They would have been prepared to take the freehold at the price we suggested - I stress the freehold - if the contents had not been dispersed. Without the contents they think the castle can't command what they call a premium."

"That's rich! It was the contents which were such a stumbling block!"

"I suggested as much."

"I hope you left them in no doubt that their offer was unacceptable."

"I did indeed. I also pointed out that it was unrealistic to include the Lodge within the reduced figure."

"Did you get the impression they're after a more advantageous lease? There could be scope for manoeuvre there, I suppose? Any views, Ricky?"

"To me the letter reads as if leasing is out of the box."

"George?"

"Yes, I am afraid that would be my view."

"George, I think Ricky and I had better talk this through. You may take it we are unlikely to play ball. A disappointing outcome. You haven't heard from any of the others we thought might be interested? The expats from Hong Kong?"

"Nothing, I'm afraid. I got the impression they found Penwhapple too remote."

"But that was the whole point! Any other interest?"

"Nothing serious. The market is very flat."

"Say nothing until you hear from me again. I feel like giving Messrs Lance and Feinstein the brush-off they deserve." Lionel picked up the receiver and replaced it, terminating the call. He checked. "Seems to have worked. So, what do you think? Tell those people to get lost?"

"I don't know, Dad. Three fifty may not be far out. There's a fully restored towerhouse in the Edinburgh area with a lower upset than that. Roughly the same accommodation as Penwhapple, according to the details. Difficult to make a proper comparison though."

"Are you implying we should take this offer seriously? You realise we lose title to the barony if we sell?"

"That could be for negotiation. It must have some commercial value - if only for the next Feinstein and Lance cook book."

"I should like you to have the title. Far be it from me to be cynical, but if you married someone with money the outlook might be different. Why don't you give Amy Wilson a call? She's your type I'd have thought. Make contact before she goes to Bristol. Lay the groundwork. I'm not an authority on matters matrimonial, I know, but it might flower into something."

"I've seen her twice since she got back from Kenya. I'm having dinner at Newhope tonight. What more am I expected to do?"

"Send her a Valentine card. Isn't that what inspirational New Man does?" Lionel unconsciously cracked the knuckles of one hand in the palm of the other, enunciating "Newhope" with some irony.

Ricky's response was unexpected. "Nice one, Dad. I'll think it over." There was just time to get a card off to Pippa. He knew the sort of thing. Victorian. Full of poetic sentiment. He'd get one for Amy as well.

"So you think we should say snap to Messrs Lance and Feinstein. A little cool bravado, in other words? You don't fancy a dram do you? I'll have one if you join me."

"At half past ten in the morning? Actually, it's not that yet. You must get a grip on your drinking, Dad. I worry about you."

"You sound like one of your aunts. We could afford to buy the others out at that ridiculous price. Mothball the castle. Keep our options open until you knew whether you wanted it. Now - whisky?"

"No way could I down a whisky at this moment. At the risk of sounding pious."

"I will pull myself together, then. You'll never know how grim life is until you've attended the Somersby budget meeting. But do you know what really gets me? It's the fact that my dear brother left the Dowery House to his widow with no strings attached. She may leave it to the Dog Home, in memory of Fogo. She's capable of anything. She makes me curse my brother. It wouldn't have been difficult to arrange for you and Tiffany to have the residual interest. And by the way, thanks for landing Tottie on me."

"You know you love Tottie." Ricky paused. "About the castle. The research I did suggests a top price of five hundred thousand, including the Lodge. Haggart's advice is in line with that. Now, these Canadians have one great merit - they actually want the place. I don't think they'll pay top price, but they'll do better than today's offer. We could probably get four fifty out of them, and keep the Lodge for ourselves. I'd settle for less, and the Lodge is negotiable as far as I'm concerned."

"Very statesmanlike. I wonder if your Cousin Tiffany would think so."

"She might."

"Know what? I shall see what George thinks."

"And I'll send Amy Wilson a Valentine card. As for Somersby, Dad, relax. It's not a drain on our resources the way Penwhapple is. It's nice having the school there. It's an interest for you."

"But the school want to move! The redoubtable Miss Spencer has a possible deal stitched up with the education people. And I can tell you something else: your Aunt Gwen is pushing the Dower House at them. She's after the Moffat money of course. What's left of it. The school could never afford what that place is worth."

"Perhaps they could rent. Aunt Gwen might be prepared to do something seriously perverted to help Miss Spencer."

"I take it you mean perverse, Ricky." Lionel walked to the window and looked at his son's car. He admired Ricky for holding onto it, when he could have made the case for a trade-in. He cracked his knuckles, thinking that love for his son had been the one constant element in his life.

Lionel arrived at the Dower House late and smelling of drink. Gwen posed herself for him in front of the alcove, with its fancy clock and glamorous studio portrait. She wore a suit which Lionel had not seen before, less severe than the neat, short-skirted ensembles she usually favoured. Her hair looked different too. Her only jewellery was a brooch of Danish silver. As usual, she reeked of perfume.

Lionel had dressed carefully. He wore his double breasted pinstripe and hand-sewn demi-brogues. He took her to a country hotel, where they ate in a panelled room like the study at Somersby. Lionel ordered a distinguished claret. The main course was excellent. Having finished it, and having emptied most of her wineglass with discriminating appreciation, Gwen said, "D'you know, you're almost as good at choosing a wine as Drummond was. Fill my glass would you, Lionel dear."

Lionel poured her more, reserving a final glass for himself. "You have coped well with living alone, Gwen," he told her. "But if I were invisible beside you at the mirror, shouldn't I perceive the brave mask slip a little?"

Gwen was not given to mourning her circumstances in commune with her reflection. Her habit was to peer keenly at it, her mind elsewhere, while she dabbed and combed. But the suggestion appealed. She denied it lightly, adding, "I imagine you have never indulged in self-pity."

"Nope."

"Do you know, Lionel, if you suddenly became a nicer man, I would be quite shocked." She patted his hand.

He locked hers in his briefly, leaning forward. "You would be more than shocked. You would be very disappointed." Then, as though calling himself to order, he cleared his throat and put his elbows on the table. "So we're thick as thieves about the castle. That's good. I have to say, Gwen, I am amazed at your insouciance over the Dower House business. Where will you go if the school move in, and you've settled for a pittance?"

"I've thought of joining my sister in Kent. I'd welcome the extra warmth of the South-East."

"Stap me vitals," said Lionel. He tilted his head at her. "Having quarrelled with her all your life?"

"I like Kent."

"Don't be ridiculous. Kent is famous for blinding snow."

She regarded him. "I always have to think twice before I speak to you, it seems." She sounded piqued, finding his changes of mood disconcerting.

"So Kent was a random shot?"

Gwen smiled submissively. "I would have expected you to say, an empty threat. Would you be sorry if I moved to Kent? Or are you too selfish?"

"Too selfish. The charm is in not denying it. Come on. Coffee and petit fours in the lounge. I don't think I could face a pudding."

"I can't take my eyes off that sweet trolley. Please order something creamy and rich, there's a dear." She glanced under her lashes at him, challenging the legendary charm.

"A pudding you shall have. This time next year you may be

a native of Kent." With affectionate contempt he watched her consume fruit gateau, his eyes following the dainty movements of her fingers as she forked it slowly to her lips. Later, in the lounge, she watched him despatch most of the petit fours, during which performance she was ignored. They kissed in the hotel car park. Then they drove briskly back to the Dower House. Gwen's skirt moved fluidly under Lionel's hand as he caressed her thigh.

Standing behind her in the sitting room, lightly fingering her neck, Lionel observed Fogo's tapestry chair. The cushion used to finish up on the floor. He drew Gwen down onto the settee and held her on his lap, one arm encircling her waist, the other resuming the exploration of her thigh. He laid his mouth against her ear, gratified by the sensation it gave him. "You murdered Drummond's dog," he whispered.

She promptly left his lap, colour filling her cheeks. "What do you mean, Lionel? Your humour can be quite offensive."

"But you did," he confirmed. His eyes took on their yellowish brightness. "I ask myself, were I to fall short, what would be my fate?"

Gwen succeeded in returning his smile. "I couldn't know you so well and not be aware of the puerile side to your character."

"Do you know what Ogier wears under his kilt?"

"Certainly not."

"It never occurred to you to wonder?" In front of his mind another puerile notion evolved. Was he even more drunk than he thought, or had he heard Fogo jumping out of the tapestry chair? He stood, went to the door and carefully straightened a framed piece of embroidery which Gwen had kept back from the Penwhapple sale.

"Darling. You've made it a tiny bit worse." Ostensibly insisting on the angle of the frame, Gwen offered him an elliptical revelation of herself.

He returned to the settee. "I acknowledge that women have unholy powers of intuition. But you don't have an inkling how hellishly miserable I've been feeling recently."

Gwen leant against him. "It's imperceptive of you not to see that I do."

He shook his head. "You are a perfect woman." He kissed her once more. "But you don't understand."

Full of persuasive dismay, she said, "Oh, but I do, dearest Lionel! I understand how depressed you are over Ricky, throwing himself at the wrong girl, as you see it." Her arms came up round him. "Of course I do."

Delicious female, if only it were that simple. He turned, pushing Gwen backwards. The hand slipped under her skirt this time. Removing her pants came next, then the cruder mechanics of sex. Almost immediately Lionel ejaculated. Gwen's legs wrapped round him, prolonging her pleasure. The disagreeable sensation that a ghostly Fogo was observing them returned. A baleful, judgmental creature, passing sentence on behalf of its dead master. The whim was hateful to Lionel for being, unlike his chosen puerilities, involuntary.

Gwen extricated herself from the cushions and, with flustered movements, gathered up her items of clothing. With a final glance expressing languor, bliss, future promise, entreaty against blame or regret, and personal, chaste contrition, she vanished to the bathroom. Lionel sat upright, absentmindedly wiping himself with a sock. By the time Gwen reappeared, her hair-do magically re-established, he was in his formal pin-stripes again. It was as though they had entered the house that moment and she had been to spend a penny.

Lionel took his turn in the bathroom. He reached down a bottle and rinsed his mouth. Silently counting ten, a cadddish thought to seal the evening occurred to him: Tottie. She would need her comfort walk. In the belief that he could never recapture the feel-good factor inwardly, or a sense of romance with any other mortal ever again, he returned to the flesh and blood mongrel bitch, with her very reasonable, uncomplicated needs. He hastened to exert his authority over her, giving her a short walk before shutting the dog, and then himself, away for the night.

Chapter 24

A price of four hundred and fifty thousand pounds was agreed for the freehold of Penwhapple Castle, including the Lodge. Lionel secured this by telling Gwen he would purchase the castle on Ricky's behalf for anything less, knowing she would brief her friends. Having sold Penwhapple, a deal with the School followed. It was to relocate to the local authority premises which Samantha had identified in Ayr. The link with the family was ended.

Ricky's partnership in Moffat and Moffats ended too. Wanting more scope, he moved to a job in Glasgow. In June he sent Pippa a card with his new address. He sent a similar card to Amy Wilson, amongst others. Amy responded with an enthusiastic letter, Pippa with a picture, drawn by herself, in pastels. It showed a flowerbed spelling the words Good Luck. This prompted Ricky to go to Somersby for the Misdsummer Festival, the last to be held before the school moved away. He slipped into Camelot just in time to hear a small boy, dressed in red, announce vehemently, "You dare think it. I dare do it!" The figure in red was Loki, God of Mischief, by far the most real of the Gods in the Norse Pantheon. The angelic looking child playing the part was young Antony Hogarth.

The Festival concluded with the traditional invitation to tea in the Mansion. Ricky decided to go in search of Pippa: he had left Tottie in the car and felt she might need a run. As he rounded the flighting pond he saw a group from Pippa's class, still in their costumes. The tree house had become Valhalla, and the Gods were squabbling for possession.

The classroom was closed. A notice advised Ricky that the College had decided to hold a single, large exhibition at the Mansion this year. Ricky decided he and Tottie might as well see Pippa's classroom anyway. His first impression was a lively jumble of last minute preparations for the play. It was a moment before Ricky realized that Antony was in the room, seated at his desk. He looked away as Ricky entered, shielding the sheet of paper on which he was working.

"Hello Childe! I thought you were at the tree house. I'll tie Tottie up, don't worry."

Ricky looped the lead over the bench outside the classroom door, disappointed by Antony's withdrawn behaviour. Returning to the room he said, "Show me what you're doing. Or is it a secret?" Shyly, Antony half revealed the picture on which he was working.

"Very good," said Ricky. "Stunning!" The drawing was of a Kalashnikov automatic rifle. "There's something missing though. D'you know what? The safety catch. Make a little hook, there. That way the gun won't go off."

Antony drew in a safety catch and showed Ricky the result.

"Now, what about some lettering? Did Aunt Sylvia teach you her Gothic script?"

"No she never did." The words were spoken without expression.

"You were lucky then. Here, get out your colours. What's your favourite colour? Mine used to be red. Can I start with red, and make some letters? Then you choose a colour."

Antony was adding a halo to Ricky's lettering when Pippa came in. He tried to hide the picture. Ricky, moving swiftly, handed it over. "It's a Kalashnikov automatic rifle," he told her. "With the safety catch on. The message is specially for you."

As Pippa struggled to decipher Ricky's version of Sylvia's Gothic script, her expression softened.

"Never. Never. Let. Your. Gun
Pointed. Be. At. Any. One."

"I agree with that, Antony. And what super writing Mr Moffat has done for you."

"It's Aunt Sylvia's writing."

"Then I shall keep this picture. We'll show it to your Mummy and Daddy. But, please, no more guns."

Antony looked at Ricky "Can I take Tottie on the lead?"

"Well, no - because I don't trust her. Just sit with her. She's very friendly." Antony went outside and sat by Tottie, who licked his face. Ricky turned back to Pippa. "Have you time for a cup of tea?"

"I've got half an hour, then I'm supervising the washing up.

Could I see you tomorrow? I'm longing to hear about Glasgow."

"I have to get back this evening. Look, why don't we give tea a miss? Let's sit on the bench outside for a while. You wouldn't mind if I kept you to myself for half an hour?"

Pippa felt like telling him she would not mind if he kept her to himself for longer than that. She encouraged him to tell her about Glasgow. They exchanged news of Tiffany. If there was a Cabinet reshuffle it seemed possible she would come back to Edinburgh. Antony tired of this adult conversation and began manoeuvering Tottie away. Ricky pulled Pippa to her feet and they all walked back to the car.

" Will you be staying with the restructured Somersby?" Ricky asked.

"I don't know. Ogier's going to the Black Isle, they're desperately short of teachers there." Her tone changed. The ex-Council premises in Ayr might interest her, if Samantha was determined to be bold. A stint with that sort of experience could be just what she needed. Or she could move to the Black Isle. What did Ricky think?

"The Black Isle! Don't even consider it."

There could have been an alternative ending to their conversation. He could have asked Pippa to marry him. Years later Ricky suspected this was what he had always wanted to do. He had been too immature. That moment on the Somersby drive might have contained the best opportunity for happiness life was to afford. With the passing of time this impression grew stronger, a nostalgic, romantic indulgence.

At the time Ricky was aware only of affectionate indifference. Antony ran off blithely to rejoin his class. Pippa thanked Ricky for his part in the picture she had been given and exclaimed, "Goodness! I hadn't realized. Is it a new car? The Glaswegian girls will be impressed. Especially with your new hair style."

"Thought you'd like that. Sharp, isn't it?"

As he leaned from the window to say good bye, she told him, "Remember to change down before you enter the corners."

"I'll try."

"Have you seen the programme for the Edinburgh Festival?"

"Yes, I seem to be on their data base for some reason."

"Study it carefully."

"I will."

"I must go. You've made me late. Stop at the end of the drive and look both ways. And Ricky - be sure to wave."

"My dear Guggums, goodbye."

"Goodbye, dear Gug."

Ricky stopped at the end of the drive, leant out again and waved. Pippa waved back. He swept onto the Girvan road. It was the last time they were to see each other. Someone Pippa recognised emerged from one of the cottages. It was Phoebe Donaldson, returning as a former star pupil. They got talking.

"Who else is going to the Black Isle then?" Phoebe asked.

"The Hogarths. Alison is terribly cut up about the move to Ayr."

"Well, I'm gutted by it. And you? Are you going to the Black Isle, or to Ayr?"

Pippa was tempted to say she would be taking up a post in a peripheral housing estate. Castlemilk would have sounded spunky. But, anxious not to be later than she was already for the washing up, she replied, "You'll find Mrs Hogarth at the Mansion. Art is on display there this year, not in the art room. Oh, look, here's Mr Boyd. He'll be so interested in your news, Phoebe. I'm not sure what I shall be doing next year, to be honest."

Ogier came forward. "Good heavens. It's Phoebe! I'm glad you're here." She was smaller than he remembered and tending to be plump. She was covered with freckles. They appealed to him. Her clothes were somewhat hippie he would have said, but she wore them well and he thought her very attractive. As Pippa left, he asked her about Robert. "Do you ever see him now?"

"Oh no." Phoebe appeared to find this funny. "I know where he is and what he's doing. But we don't meet up." She was curious to hear why he was selling Somersby and moving North. What was the point of having a school in Ayr? The whole point of Somersby was the country environment.

"It wasn't my decision to make." Ogier tried to explain the shift in responsibilities, the fact that Somersby did not belong to him.

"Well, I'm absolutely gutted," Phoebe told him. Then she laughed. She seemed very happy.

"Did I hear you talking to Miss Cursiter about your fifth year project? Before the Battle, wasn't it? I know Mrs Hogarth considered it one of the best things you did."

Phoebe ransacked her memory.

"I wonder if you took my advice and kept it."

"Oh yes! That!" A flush crept over Phoebe's face. Ogier felt he must be be blushing too. He recollected his suspicion that Phoebe had modelled the lady on Pippa, the knight quite possibly on himself. Phoebe laughed self-consciously. "D'you know what I was trying to do with that picture? I was imagining myself as the person tying the ribbons and Robert as the kneeling knight! I was so embarrassed in case he found out. I don't think I meant it seriously. More a kind of spoof."

"And did you keep it?"

"I don't know. I don't think so."

It was astonishing how disappointed Ogier felt. "I hope you didn't chuck all your art away. In years to come, perhaps when you have children, you'll be surprised how things like your fifth year project will bring it all back. Robert or no Robert."

"What d'you mean, Robert or no Robert?" Phoebe opened her eyes playfully at him.

Ogier found it necessary to check his watch. He gave Phoebe a forced smile. "Now have some tea and do talk to Alison Hogarth. She really admired your work."

That night, when all was quiet, Ogier sat in the big window of the staff room and watched the Midsummer bonfire being lit. Even at this late hour the sky was not quite dark. He imagined Pippa walking arm in arm with Tiffany across the home park, as if nothing need ever change. A fresh start, thought Ogier. At my age, a fresh start.

Behind him was the capstan table for which he had fought so hard. It would go to Ayr now, where it would probably be sold to raise funds for the new school. Samantha had made it clear that sacrifices would be necessary. He must write to Tiffany, warn her that her idea of setting up a trust fund would not work in the way she expected. The bonfire had still to catch properly. Ogier felt a painful clash of loyalties.

Across the park a figure was making its way back to the house, heading for the gate beside the copper beech tree. Perhaps it was Pippa. The Entry into Valhalla, which her class had performed that afternoon, had been good. Pippa's enthusiasm had communicated itself, the children had experienced the myth's inner reality. It had shown insight to cast Antony Hogarth as Loki. The boy was coming into himself, getting his confidence back. And perhaps Tiffany would see her destiny as a teacher after all.

Suddenly the fire blazed up. The brushwood on the lee side must have kindled. It was always a dramatic moment when the brushwood caught. In the sudden brightness it was Valhalla which Ogier saw, a great, golden castle, ardently creative, an ideal place, Bryony's Joyous Guard.

Chapter 25

The week before Parliament rose in July was difficult. Even Lord Venables became short tempered. Then the Session was over. MPs dispersed to their constituencies, Ministers went on holiday. The Cabinet reshuffle was not now expected until the Autumn. Tiffany, part of the skeleton staff left in London, found herself at a loose end.

She kept to her usual routine of coming in early, without breakfast. She made herself a cup of black instant coffee and read the day's papers. That took her until half past eight. Today there were a couple of points she wanted to discuss with colleagues in Edinburgh. That took her until nine. She wandered through to the Ministerial offices, to see if the Secretariat were expecting problems. This was good for a laugh. By nine thirty she was back at her desk with nothing to do.

She felt famished. Since Iona's death Tiffany had been losing weight.

Her office was on the first floor, in one of the wings overlooking what had been the entrance courtyard. She shared it with two others, which suited her sociable temperament. The table on which the daily papers were spread was in this room, as was the TV monitor. There was seldom a dull moment. Today she was on her own. The dull moments extended into hours. The weather was hot, the office airless. Two difficult letters had come for Tiffany in the week before the Recess, one from Haggarts, the other from Samantha. She had tried to deal with them more than once. She needed space. She had it now.

First, Haggarts. A longish letter, containing a Trust Deed for Tiffany to execute in favour of Somersby School. It provided for wide discretion to be exercised by the College of Teachers. In a covering letter George Haggart reminded her of his earlier advice that safeguards were desirable. Quixotically determined to honour her Aunt's memory, Tiffany's plans had become increasingly ambitious. A substantial sum was now involved - her entire legacy from Sylvia, including her share of the money for the Rossetti.

'Disbursements to be made only with the written agreement of yourself or your nominated representatives.'

Tiffany read these words with a troubled frown. Surely the family connection with Somersby was safeguard enough. George Haggart was covering himself. Tiffany sensed treachery and self-interest.

Samantha's letter. Again, perfectly positive on the face of things, but with the real meaning occluded.

'Dear Tiffany.'

This was typed. The Information Directorate's practice was for the superscription to be added by hand.

'Thanks to careful advance planning, it is now certain that New Somersby will complete its move to Ayr in time for Christmas, a remarkable and exciting achievement. To make sure we continue to carry parents and supporters with us in the longer term, and as an aid to fund-raising, we are establishing a widely based Council in which matters of strategy can be addressed. New Somersby is to be a school for the many, not the few. There has been some speculation that it might become a school for girls only. It is true that the Upper School in particular has always attracted a strong entry from able girls, while the appeal to boys has been less consistent. The Trustees believe it should be possible to play to this strength, while of course putting the interests of existing pupils first. This is the sort of issue which could hopefully be discussed in a wider forum of the kind now proposed.'

The Trustees! The Council. Nothing about the College of Teachers. The ungrammatical 'hopefully!'

'I stress that the Council, if it is established, will not have any executive powers in relation to the new Board of Trustees.'

The Council again.

'It would act in an advisory capacity. However the intention would be for the Council to make an important contribution to the development of New Somersby, and my purpose in writing now is to invite you to become a founding member. I do hope you will find it possible to serve.'

There was more: draft terms of reference, guidelines for members. And then there was Samantha's separate, handwritten postscript:

'We are so heartened by your intention to establish the Sylvia Moffat Trust. You will know best what your Aunt may have intended but, quite frankly, the most effective way of helping Somersby would be a capital donation. This would respond to the perceived educational priorities of the new Trustees. I hope you like the idea of the Council. Between ourselves, the long-term aim is for this to become the shareholder body, with Trustees as an executive committee. So you will see why we want a hand-picked membership – and why you in particular would be so welcome there.'

Tiffany was getting a headache. She was also feeling restless. She was hungry but it was not food she wanted. Of the two letters, Samantha's postscript was the trickiest part. Tiffany paused for reflection, gazing at the neatly presented text from George Haggart. Into her memory drifted the awful occasion at the Dower House, when her Uncle had wanted to alter his will in her favour, his efforts to speak, and the old family lawyer attentively listening. Dear Mr Haggart. He had thought so highly of her uncle, he had never failed to express his concern and support. She must be courteous and correct with him, as Uncle Drummond would have wished.

In a clear space at the top of George Haggart's letter she laboriously inscribed a tick and sat back, surprised by the relief this small action brought. Was a single tick enough? She forced her eyes to the letter again, searching the text. Opposite the reference to 'safeguards' she placed another tick. The rest would have to wait. Beneath the tick at the head of the page Tiffany inscribed the date, and put the paper aside.

On Samantha's letter she then wrote, 'See letter of even date from GH,' and dated that.

Still a dreadful feeling of impatience. She needed to get out of this airless office.

Of course. The Council.

The women of the Moffat family had the troubling gift of clairvoyance, and feared it. Again Tiffany forced her eyes to the letter before her, found the reference she wanted and underlined it:

'I do hope you will find it possible to serve.'

Opposite that, in the margin, she inscribed a cross.

During a long and painful wait Sylvia and Drummond were palpably close to her, waiting too. With them, a third attentive figure. Her mother had joined them. The sense of loss was terrible.

Tiffany confronted her feelings for 'New' Somersby. It was the old Somersby she loved, Ogier's Somersby. Summoning her courage, she underlined her little cross, and then underlined it again. The images of death faded. There was work to do.

Tiffany got up from her desk and walked down the back stairs, avoiding the Ministerial offices. She went through the door at the back of the rotunda, around the foot of the geometric stairway and out by the main entrance. It was important to seem absolutely normal to the security guard. There had been a failure of love. A failure of love for the past. As a result, a failure in self-esteem and, as a further result, a failure in love for the future. Why had she treasured her virginity, if not because she wanted to love and be loved?

She told the security guards she was going to save Somersby School in South Ayrshire.

Her headache ought to be better. The main staircase usually made her feel jaunty. It was said to be a superlative example of Regency architecture. There was a bust of Sir Walter Scott on the landing.

She crossed Whitehall by the Cenotaph, surprised at how empty the carriageway was, even more surprised when, suddenly, it was no longer empty after all. She walked towards Parliament Square, pausing at the traffic lights. She had remembered her briefcase, not that she was expected in the House. Parliament was in Recess, she reminded herself. She walked up Bridge Street and turned into the underground station, bought a ticket and examined the map. Someone had changed Ealing Broadway to Fealing Broadway, East Putney to Breast Putney, Osterley to Posterley for Christmas. She caught her train.

Exactly six stops.

The feeling of impatience became stronger at each station. By the time the train reached Monument her headache was worse, the excitement unbearable. She got out eagerly and looked around.

Ogier was not there to meet her.

She waited until the next train came in.

No-one.

She waited where she was until the platform had cleared. People kept wandering down. She was being watched.

She positioned herself nearer the exit barrier. Two more trains, and still no Ogier. She walked back to the end of the platform.

Holding her briefcase carefully, she got down on to the track and walked into the tunnel. She knew she must avoid the live rail. A train came by. She leant against the wall of the tunnel. Another train came by. She reached an open space where tracks intersected. Ahead of her and to her left, in a twilit zone, the derelict chapel loomed. A number of levers had been installed there by occult powers.

She picked her way across the intervening tracks and clambered into the once holy building. Masterfully she operated the levers, one by one. She worked them until she was exhausted.

Several more trains went by. She waved gaily as they passed.

The levers seemed to have been disconnected. She had made a mistake. Perhaps it was not an endowment for Somersby that her Aunt Sylvia wanted but an educational trust for the Childe. It was of the utmost urgency to correct the instructions she had sent George Haggart.

She opened her briefcase and could not find his letter. But she found her diary. Frantically she scribbled a note to herself. When she checked what she had written she could not understand a word.

A two-coach train came up to the chapel and stopped. Three men got out. She hurried to the one who looked like her Uncle Drummond and told him she needed to get a letter to Haggarts in Ayr. But she could not remember the address.

Uncle Drummond put an arm round her, promising that everything would be all right. She told him there was a need for prompt action. Ogier had been beguiled. They got into the two-coach train. She sat very close to her Uncle Drummond, laid her head on his shoulder and began to cry. She told him about the worry of presenting her own TV programme.

"Cheer up. Everything will turn out fine."

He was holding her. She tried to struggle. The abattoir men moved quickly forwards. She shut her eyes and felt a heavy calm descending. She saw Ogier waving and starting to walk back to Somersby. Tiffany was struck by his face, which wore the happiest of expressions. But it was a deception. Ogier was not there. He had turned his back on Penwhapple and escaped to the Black Isle, leaving her alone, with darkness closing.

Lightning Source UK Ltd.
Milton Keynes UK
17 August 2010

158545UK00001B/87/P

9 780955 219924